FOSSIL COVE PRESS

CRAWLING TO THE MOON

And Other Stories

by

Scott Ellis

CRAWLING TO THE MOON and other stories

FOSSIL COVE PRESS, *Winnipeg, Manitoba*

Fossil Cove Publishing
Suite 1301, 90 Garry Street
Winnipeg, Manitoba, Canada, R3C 4J4
D.G. Valdron, Editor

Cover: Dawne Dominique, based on the story, The New People

Issued in electronic, print and audio formats
ISBN: 978-1-990860-42-3 (print/ trade paperback); ISBN: 978-1-990860-34-8 (Ebook); ISBN: 978-1-990860-35-5 (audio book).

Set in Garamond

Dedication

None of this work would have been possible without the constant care, organizing ability and many heroisms, large and small, of my wife Anna, who for years has done far more than her fair share to keep our household together and healthy. Anna, I can never thank you enough.

The Ellis mob, including exes and semi-Ellises, past and present, and their associated crime families also had roles in producing all this: Don, Pat, Brian, Matt, Jen, Charlotte, Leon, Margaret, Miles, Robin, Rory, Ian, Ava, Juliette, Freya, another Matt, Davis, Karen, Nancy, Jim, David, Greg and a bunch of others: There would be no me without all of you.

Friends: To Herb F., a skeptic's skeptic, an utterly decent person who makes nerd a title of honor. To Laura, who is far more competent and better company than she realizes. Peter D., gifted explainer, whose sheer intellectual stamina leaves me awestruck. To Al R., an inexhaustible source of ideas, and a constant reminder that words are only one way to make a world. Patrick L., who, without pretension, can always be relied upon to bring out the moral dimension in all actions. Phyllis and Larry C., boon companions and guides to what's behind the scenes in everyday events.

And a host of others, role models, horrible examples, troublesome heroes, gifted kvetchers, conspiracy theorists and inspired goofballs, who gave me more than I will ever completely understand.

CRAWLING TO THE MOON
And Other Stories
Table of Contents

CRAWLING TO THE MOON

There's a lemon sherbet moon sailing over the horse show stalls and palm trees and I wish I was up there, not sweat-burned and sleep-starved, tracking a dumb stallion through a steamy Florida night. It's 3 AM and every ten minutes the radio squawks a tornado warning. My ribs ache and the air's tight as a fat banker's wallet. The showground lights never stop buzzing, blazing gas trying to bust out, moths and junebugs trying to crash in. I hear horses nickering, dreaming of wither-smashing jumps or just wandering around after they bust through their flimsy, temporary stalls. Somewhere behind me Pedro is singing, full of dust, telling God all about it, "*Dios mio, mi corazon, mi puta,*" while the guys in the End Times Poker Tent call their bets and yell at him to shut up. The crickets grind out "money-money-money", two drunken Saudi princes are cursing each other in Arabic that sounds like lawnmowers eating typewriters and every breath is a leech in your lungs.

We're wandering in the dark between stables, passing a joint, looking for Biscayne, our ten million dollar palamino stud jumper, us grooms, me and Huong. Werther-Bob the Doberman's along, he says to track, though mostly he seems to be watching Huong and me. Biscayne's out there with the other sleepwalking horses who've stumbled through the ticky-tack loblolly pine boards of their stalls, vague and spooked as bad dreams.

"We'll find him," Werther-Bob grunts, scratching his ear with his hind paw, "when he figure out he jes' a horse. Night like this, everything gets jumpy. Even rich folks--every winter they bring all their top horses here and you'd think they'd be in Heaven-- surrounded by guards and other rich people. All their show horses, all that tax-shelter money in pretty saddles and tack, doin' cute little tricks where can't no sloppy-ass government get at it. Instead, they feel like they're missing somethin'--somethin' they really need. An' dumb as he is, a horse is way more attuned than any stockbroker or cocaine trafficker. It's the heat--it just keeps pushing at a nag like Biscayne, like he's got more gettin' born to do. All slicked up and can't breathe and he figures there's gotta be something more. But he'll learn. Either that, or he'll get horny."

"Dogs ever get anxious like that?" I ask.

Werther-Bob gives me his pedigreed killer grin, which looks even crazier around a spliff. "Depends. Some sorry-ass mutts, sure, all the time. But when you a Dobie, you know there ain't nothin' better than that."

"Uh huh. How come I saw you sniffing round that Shar Pei the other day?"

"Hey, noblesse oblige, Bubba." He always calls me that, though my name's Carl. One Kraut's enough around here, he says. "Even ugly bitches need somethin' to dream about."

"Yeah right. I know desperation when I see it. The way they've got you chained up all day, you'd fuck a rattlesnake."

"Depends on which end, Bubba. Maybe you be sleepin' in that shithole trailer of yours and wake up with a little touch of Dobie in the night. Anything could happen, in a tornado low."

"This good worm weather," Huong says, absently working saddle soap into one of the bridles he always carries. The thick arms and big hands incongruously stuck on his slight frame are always busy, repairing one piece of tack or another. "When I first come this country, I on worm crew. They take us out in back of truck, at night. Put little baskets on our legs. Wear hat with light on it. We run across rich people lawns, quick-quick like ghosts, take they worms. Bent over like in rice paddy. Sprinklers all time hiss like silver snake. Pick-pick at grass soft like carpet. Worms go up when moon yellow and fat like Buddha. They twist up into air and don't even know. Crawl right into sky. To the moon."

Werther-Bob snorts. "Lotta tall talk outa' stoop labor for some bait shop." Anytime they're together, the dog stares at him with predatory focus. I've slowly realized there's a chill between them, something deep and bitter. But I've been too busy working like a navvy, mucking out stalls, feeding and watering, leading horses,

Crawling to the Moon, Page 2

washing them, tacking them up and rubbing them down, to pay much mind. And somewhere along the line, I learned not to ask idle questions.

"You better hope horses can't do that. That might be Biscayne now," I say, trying to break the tension, nodding at a horse ambling between stables at the far end of the showgrounds, ambling around palmettos, toward the perimeter road.

Werther-Bob takes a sniff. "Naw, that's old Chockablock out of Triple T stables. Well, come on, let's do the neighborly thing and go collect the sucker."

"Triple T?" I say. "Let Pedro catch him, instead of getting bent and hanging around the poker game."

"Bubba," calls Werther-Bob over his shoulder, as he casually sidles over to cut the gelding off before it makes the back gate, "you got to learn the Code of the Show. Hep out a brother in need."

"Aw, fuck a whole bunch of that shit, man," I gripe while Huong and I follow his lead, angling in on the horse. "Ain't no code here. The last three weeks I been run off my ass till way past dark, for damn near minimum wage. Up at five, braiding manes, mucking stalls and getting pissed on by a bunch of landsharks, narco-kings and Eurotrash dickweeds."

The gelding isn't really trying to get away and he certainly doesn't want to go anywhere near Werther-Bob. He seems relieved when Huong strokes his neck and slips the halter on. "And first time I saw Pedro, he pulled a knife on me. Even if I did care about him losing his pissy job, why would I bring him a horse? He's so dusted up, he'd probably kill it. Brother, my ass."

"Boy, that's the thinking that landed you inside."

"Oh great, now I'm getting lectured on the karmic economy of my three-joint bust by someone who spends his days chained up with a spiked collar. I'm going to bed. The Boss can kiss my ass or fire it, I don't care which." I try to say this casually, but really I don't even like talking about the Boss, let alone dealing with him.

Just then, of course, my cell phone chirps and I jump like that time a pony bit me on the butt. It's the Boss. Shrugging like it's no big thing I lay it on the ground for Werther-Bob to talk to, like I always do.

I can't hear what they're saying, which is just fine by me. I've only ever talked to the Boss once or twice since he hired me. Or maybe it was just him talking to me, because I don't remember saying anything. I forget things. Whatever it was he said, it didn't do my state of mind no good. The Boss gives me the night sweats.

Then Werther-Bob glances over and says "He wants to talk to you."

Great, just great. I pick up the phone like it might bite me. "Yes sir?"

The Boss's voice sounds like it was boiled dry and frozen hard. "Carl," he says, making my name sound like chill wind hurtling down a gully, "are you going to find my stallion?"

"Yes sir. You bet."

There's a noise like radio static and I realize the Boss is laughing. "That's right, I bet. I want you to know, Carl, that there's a lot riding on that horse. He's at the crest of the standing wave. There's instability in the field and Biscayne is a pivot point. But I don't need to tell you that."

I'm not sure what the Boss thinks I know, but it ain't anything close to what he's talking about. I nod, as if he could see me, because I don't know what to say. I can hear the End Time Poker Game in the background. I don't know how those voices sound so cold and quiet and echo-y, when they're all sitting in a big tent in the steamy night not a quarter mile away.

Then the Boss says "Good," like he's seen my nod and we've made an agreement, only not what I think it is. "I know I can count on you. Now listen, Carl, there's a lot things in the wind tonight. If something happens and Werther-Bob can't get here, I need you to come tell me right away. Do you understand?"

That much I get, though it's the last thing I want to do. "I understand, sir, " I say, wracking my brains to find some kind of out, "but what about Pedro? He's all lit up on PCP and he's got a knife."

"You won't have any trouble with him. Just make sure you come if anything happens." He hangs up, leaving me with one more lovely thing to look forward to.

"Oh great. Now I got the Boss on my case, like I need something else to sweat."

"Rest easy, Bubba," Werther-Bob says. "The thing he's worried about, it ain't gonna happen."

"You're sure about that, huh? Whatever-the-hell thing he's talking about, there ain't a chance in the world, according to you."

"Boy, look around you. This horse show system's been running way before you came and it'll be here when you're long gone. It ain't like nobody's tried to screw it up before. Hell, the Owners do a damn good job themselves, what with packin' billions of dollars worth of horseflesh into stalls that won't stand up to a hard sneeze. You'd think they want to bring it all down. Who knows, maybe they do. The Boss 'n' them, they been at it a long time, and that'll change even an Owner. But you and me, Bubba, we're going to make sure that don't happen." He lunges forward, suddenly and his forepaws thud down on my shoulders. His breath is foul with old meat and his white teeth too near my face. "Just you keep in mind, son, there's scarier things around than Pedro." He drops down, gives me a wink and I can almost breathe again.

"He is ghost," Huong says, passing Chockablock's lead rope to me and nodding back in the general direction of the End Times Poker Game. The gelding nickers uncertainly and he strokes its nose. Huong says the damnedest things sometimes. I thought he was from one of the Vietnamese hill tribes originally, but I met a waitress from Ho Chi Minh City who said he had to be from somewhere else, she didn't know where. Huong doesn't say. Got the easiest hand with horses I've ever seen, though.

The Boss is in the game and Pedro is hanging around the tent outside, so Werther-Bob is a bit confused, something that doesn't happen often. "Pedro, a ghost? Naw, he's just like the rest of you piss-smelling, two-leg gimps. Wears trousers he gotta put on, one leg at a time."

"According to Huong's people, all us roundeyes are ghosts. Right, Huong?" He nods.

"Zat a fact?" Werther-Bob is intrigued. "So am I, like, a ghost dog?" he asks, staring at the small man, and I suddenly realize I've never seen him address Huong directly before.

"You number-one ghost dog."

"That's some shit, huh, Bubba? The Phantom Dobie: You can't hear him, you can't see him, till he got his jaws upside your gizzard."

"Yeah, WB, just what you want on the ol' resume. In the attaché case you'll be toting everywhere, once we get the opposable thumb thing licked."

"Fuck you, Carl, and every other limp-dick, Wisconsin cheesehead."

Crawling to the Moon, Page 5

"Hey, at least I don't have the papers to prove I'm inbred."

"Keep on talking, boy, an' they gon' be one less mutt out here."

I ignore him, which just shows how far gone I am. I once saw Werther-Bob wake from a light doze and kill a big raccoon that was nosing around for scraps, all in less time than it takes to say. It's the heat--It does things to your judgment. I swipe the sweat out of my eyes. "So, if we're all ghosts, Huong, how come you pointed out Pedro special?"

"Number-ten ghost. Ghost of ghost." He gives one of his schoolgirl giggles. Then stops, holds his big, strangely smooth hands up in the air and brings them, cupped, towards his pug nose. He stops walking, then whistles low under his breath, a thing I've never heard him do before. "Something happen."

Werther-Bob glances at Huong, suddenly alert. He takes a sniff. His eyes widen and he draws in a lungful. "Oh shit."

"What? What's happening?" They're both staring off somewhere, up, like they're watching a comet come whizzing in to destroy the earth or something. Whatever's between them is thicker now, almost visible. The air is quiet, as if everything just decided to inhale.

Werther-Bob shakes himself and growls "Huong, see if you can rouse Cappy and Art over at Coral Gates. Y'all get li'l Miss Debutante out on I-49 up to Tampa."

Huong hesitates, as if torn by some longing. Without warning, WB springs at the slight man, knocking him flat. Bristling, he snarls down into the brown, fine-boned face, "Don't get no cute ideas, you phony-ass gook. You know what you signed on for." Huong stares impassively up at the long row of glinting teeth. Somehow, he doesn't seem to be the one being threatened. But he nods.

Werther-Bob sighs and I'd swear he's relieved. Then he backs off, staring to the side, while Huong picks himself up and starts to trot back toward the showground gates. For once, the Doberman seems at a loss. "While you're doing that," he calls after Huong, awkwardly, "I'll go bark at the poker game."

I clear my throat. "Not that it's any of my business, but..."

It's a wonder to me how there can be such a mixture of relief, contempt and perilous affection in a killer's pointed glance. He chuckles and I have a rush of fury, what you feel toward someone who is way ahead of you and doesn't care. Luckily before I say something dumb, he explains, "There's a mare gone into heat early, oh, I'd say 'bout a quarter mile southeast of here. Prolly that dizzy little sorrel hunter up at R&T stable, I don't miss my guess. Huong's going to try and get her into a trailer, downwind, before she has her big moment way too soon. You go on ahead and try to get as many guys as you can back here to hold Biscayne." He starts to trot off.

"What about this guy?" I nod at the gelding, who's gone from a sweated loginess to the dancing hysteria of a horse ready to bolt. His eyes roll and he shies when I take hold of his bridle, holding him close.

"Tie him up somewheres. You got more important things to do."

"How do you know Biscayne's coming this way?"

Werther-Bob pauses, looking back over his shoulder. That flesh-tearing grin again. "If he don't come through here, you'll know where he is anyway. Once he get a sniff, won't be but one thing on his mind. He gon' be nothin' but 18 hunnert pound of boner, comin' at that filly on a bee-line." Then he boots it, that whip-spine wolf sprint. He's halfway to the poker tent before I can say anything else.

And there I am, alone with a horse that ain't my business, with nothing but some vague orders to gather up some guys I don't know, some of whom are right now guaranteed whacked out of their skulls on angel dust and Lord knows what else. Owners are weird, riders are nasty, muscle is scary, but some grooms will flat out kill you, for no particular reason. I look up at the moon. It sure seems cool and sweet, sailing up there where nobody can get at you. Staring at it too long is a bad idea, though. I start to get the memories, the ones that make my head hurt, where my back is cold because the prison yard concrete is sucking out all the heat and I can see Tariq Johnson wiping off the filed-down rat-tail comb he just stabbed me with and the white-gold searchlight keeps pulling at me, drawing me up...

Behind me a couple of 1x4's snap and there's Biscayne, lathered up and ready to rock, coming right through the fence. I call him, but he doesn't even turn to look. I know I should get ahead of him, but I'm rooted to the ground. Maybe it's the golden, streaky glow of him. Or his breathing, hoarse and fast, or bloodshot eyes, or the chewing way his mouth is working. Maybe it's just the mean-looking dong on him, hanging halfway to the ground. I don't know.

I know what finally gets me moving: It's the smell of thrush coming from his hooves. I pull the cleaning hook out of my back pocket, moving to cut him off. Damn, I think, watching Biscayne's clinking feet, smelling the oily-sweet decay, I thought I cleaned all that stuff out this morning.

Still calling, I move toward the stallion, sidling in, wondering what I'm going to do if he charges. Werther-Bob barks in the distance. I vaguely realize I've never heard him do that before. Biscayne snorts when I get too close, slow-dancing away in a cross-legged shuffle, like he's in some phantom dressage exercise, while cicadas and tree   frogs throb for each other and twisting bat shadows swoop up junebugs under malarial stadium lights. I can't head him off or even really see him well. He seems to fade in and out in the moonlight and the shadows of stables and trees. But I stumble along, scratching where I've already got a rash from no-see-um bites, trying to follow the smell. I catch a glimpse of him, disappearing around a stable corner off to my left.

There's a rush of hard paws behind me and Werther-Bob is back. "The guys are coming," he says. "Where's our stud?"

"He just turned that corner." I point.

"King Jesus jump down, Bubba," the Doberman snarls. "You was supposed to stay ahead of him. Leastways, keep his ass in sight."

"He was too skittish to catch. Kept shying away." It sounds lame, even to me. "What happened to this bee-line stuff you were talking about?" I ask, trying to rally.

"Wind's shifted, is all. He's lost the scent." The dog trots off toward the stable, then stops, summoning me with a peremptory nod. "C'mon boy, for once in your half-bright life, do the smart thing and protect the Boss's investment. Not to mention yo' no-account butt." Is it my imagination, or does Werther-Bob sound worried?

"What wind?" I carp, grudgingly falling into step. "It's dead calm. I only wish there was a--"

And from nowhere there is a cool gust of breeze, so fragrant with rain and ocean I can almost see the blue sweetness of it. Faint thunder rolls in, on the hooves of a great, faraway herd.

"How's he do that?" I wonder out loud, as Werther-Bob disappears round a corner.

"If I got to explain it, Bubba, you ain't never gon' know," the answer floats back to me. The dog favors me with a cold grin when I catch up, "Your sorry ass might just have caught a break, boy. Thought I just saw ol' Biscayne mosey right into our stable. Maybe he's back in his stall, chowin' down on sweet feed right now. Don't count on it, though." He nods toward the aisle between stalls, where great dim shapes mill in the dark. "Y'all go inside and check."

"How come you never go inside, WB? What are you, horse-shy?"

He sighs, turns to me and I catch a glimpse of his huge, taxed patience. "Horses go crazy when I come too close, Bubba," he says quietly. "Not all of them right away, but it don't do none of them no good."

"There are dogs in lots of stables."

"Carl, you a nice kid, even if you ain't the sharpest tool in the shed. But sometime even a nice kid like you got to consider the ramifications of yo' employment situation. I ain't no regular dog. And you ain't workin' for no average Boss."

The wind picks up as we approach the big, low building and I hear thunder from another direction, the way a storm plays as it stalks you. For some reason I don't want to go into the stable. "See, you're always hinting around about that stuff, but you never just tell me how come you can--"

"I tol' you, I owe the Boss."

"But--"

"There are Powers in the Darkness, Bubba. Dominions, Thrones and Principalities. Then there's fuckups like you. Now git."

The stable is full of gold moonlight on the straw. The clouds haven't moved in yet. For some reason the horses are quiet. Storm weather usually spooks them. I count them again. Only Biscayne missing. Candycorn, our little Quarter-Arab hunter, gives me a velvety nuzzle as I pass.

I jump when someone taps me on the shoulder. I hate the way Huong does that. People should make some noise when they come up behind you. I'm about to give him a blast as I turn.

It's a girl I haven't seen before. She's slim and tan and taller than I am, a bit, in tight, faded jeans and a plaid shirt tied off so it's like a halter top. She's got a battered old straw fedora parked on a mass of tangled blond dreadlocks. She grins and says "Sorry I spooked you." One of her front teeth is chipped. Apart from that she's beautiful, the kind you find yourself backing away from, it makes you so nervous.

"Um, that's okay."

"Becky O'Leary." She holds out a long hand, which I take because I don't know what else to do. Even in mucking out clothes, she smells like money. On the horse show circuit, the best thing a groom can usually do is get himself ignored.

Werther-Bob explained it to me once. It's actually the first thing I remember since I hitched a ride with him and the Boss. I forget a lot of things. He said "Bubba, round here there are five Orders of Being: Owners, Riders, Muscle, Mounts and pissant Grooms like you. You smart, you'll stay clear of the first three and tend to the fourth."

He was right, too. Here at the show there's European, Arab and Texas royalty, mafiosi, cocalistas and every kind of margin-shaving, ambulance-chasing, blood-sucking yuppie. There are your Riders, a bunch of bulimic, coke-hoovering prima donnas. Then there are the big dudes in mirrored shades and specially-tailored suits who watch you all the time they talk into their lapels, plus all the chained up rottweilers, shepherds and dobermans. Each and every one a nasty piece of work. I been spit on, threatened and cut dead in every way but actually and I ain't even been here long. At least I think I haven't. Like I said, I forget things.

So I'm careful what I say to this girl. "What can I do for you, Miss O'Leary?"

"Becky. Could you help me find my horse? She's a white Barb. Goes by Sweet Selena. I thought I saw her come in here."

Now somehow this just strikes me as a bald-faced lie, but I keep my face still. I also wonder how Werther-Bob could have thought Biscayne had come back here. He knows his horses. Anyways, if that stallion's on the prowl, every last one of our other horses would be worked up and spooked if he'd even come close. These guys here are calm and quiet, like they were back home on a drowsy country night, instead of jammed into ticky-tack stalls with a tornado just waiting to happen and all these loony, somnambulant horses, all these guys with guns and walkie-talkies, all these tweaked out grooms, all this lunatic money running around.

"Sure thing, Miss O'Leary," I say. "I got another horse to look for anyway."

She starts to say "Becky" again, then stops and nods to herself. "Biscayne, right?"

"You seen him?"

"I thought I might've. Over by the sinkhole."

"Aw, Jesus."

The sinkhole is the last place you want your horse to wander. It'd be bad enough if it were just like other sinkholes, a place where the soft limestone that makes up most of Florida had collapsed due to a lowered water table. But the way this particular one had fallen in had heaved up a wedge of harder rock on a steep angle. The Slippery Slope, the locals call it and it is. They've roped it off for the duration of the Show, but there are always grooms and hustlers up there smoking joints laced with PCP, supposedly-banned horse tranquilizer everyone has on hand.

Becky says "C'mon, I'll help you look. I've got a feeling we'll find Biscayne and Selena close together."

"Sure, I guess..." I don't ask why she thinks this. Something weird about this chick. She's a Rider no doubt, maybe even an Owner. Now sometimes, you catch them alone, they're friendly enough, like they might actually breathe the same air as you do. But this feels different. The scar on my left ribs starts to itch.

So we go out into the night. The wind's picked up and there's no mistaking the tornado lurking around somewhere. It's not like a hurricane. Hurricanes ain't sneaky. They come in from hundreds of miles out to sea, where you can keep an eye on them. But a tornado will pop out of stuff that was just minding its own business last time you looked. It's like everything has a twister in it somewhere and only needs a nudge to bust it loose.

Getting out of the stable is kind of a relief. I can feel the sweat cool me where there's finally a breeze to dry it. Even the crickets and the peepers seem to calm down a bit.

I got to trot to keep up with Becky, though. Usually you kind of stroll through the showgrounds, catch a horse here, or there, maybe bullshit with some other grooms if they ain't too bent, ask if they've seen your horse, tell them where you caught sight of theirs. But she really motors toward the sinkhole. Sails right by those two Saudi princes Hamid and Mahfooz, now drunkenly propping each other up. They don't even glance at her, which is weird considering both these jerks thinks he's God's Gift. Passes right by Chips Ahoy, a bay hunter-jumper out of Coral Gables and doesn't even glance at him.

Maybe this is a good thing. Last thing I need to do is catch Hell from the Boss because his ten mil stud jumper's broken his neck, or drowned or something.

We turn the corner past the big live oak and there's Sweet Selena, the prettiest little mare you ever did see, all silver in the moonlight, grazing in a little hollow beside a willow tree. Somehow, it's like she was waiting for us.

Not that she's all that easy to approach. She's all lathered up, keeps dancing around and flicking her tail up. Maybe she smells Biscayne. Maybe it's just the tornado low that's got her spooked. She whinnies and shies whenever I come near.

Becky just keeps talking to her, crooning really, like you half-sing kids to sleep. I can't make out the words.

This girl really has the touch with horses. In a minute or two, Becky's stroking that soft pink muzzle. Then she hops up on Selena's back and clucks gently. The mare starts to amble out of the clearing and I figure that's the last I'll see of them.

But when she's about to pass me, she stops and holds out a hand. "Jump on, Carl," she says.

First of all, I don't recall ever telling her my name. Riders don't generally care, unless you're working for them and sometimes not even then.

The other thing is that no one here has ever offered me a ride on their horse. It just isn't done. Werther-Bob explained it to me once, just after I'd hitched a ride with him and the Boss and got hired. I was glad to get out of that semi cab, wondering how it could be so dark in there when it was glaring Florida midday outside. I don't recall ever saying I wanted the job, but then, like I said, I forget things. Anyway, I was hired and I knew it.

I'd told Werther-Bob I had ridden horses on my grandpa's farm, back in Wisconsin. He stopped me right there. "Thing is, Bubba," he said, "these horses are worth more than you're ever gonna see in your life and they're trained a certain way. You don't wanna mess with that. Besides, you're a Groom now and Grooms don't ride. It'd be like putting a piece of glass from a graduation ring in a platinum setting."

So I'm hesitant.

Becky doesn't seem to care, though. "C'mon," she says. "What have you got to lose?"

While I'm thinking about that she grabs my shoulders and hauls me on in front of her. She's stronger than she looks, is all that occurs to me at the time. Which just goes to show how out of it I am. I don't even notice how she manages this without benefit of stirrups or even a saddle.

Now that I'm up, I wonder how long it's been since I rode. Seems like decades. Sometimes I can't remember nothing but mucking out stalls, cleaning hooves, rubbing down and bandaging legs.

I'm just getting used to being up there, the broad, smooth weight and muscle between my legs, hard little rich girl tits pressing into my back, when Becky says "Why do you think you're here, Carl?"

I hate when people ask me questions like that. I'm here because I got out of prison and this is the first job I could find. Out loud I say "Well ma'am, it's a horse show. You gotta have it somewhere, I guess."

"No, but how did you get here?"

"I was hitching a ride and the Boss and Werther-Bob picked me up and hired me."

"Werther-Bob, that'd be the Doberman you talk to, right? And once she says it, it sounds flat-out crazy. I suddenly remember being somewhere where you didn't talk to dogs. Or at least if you did, they wouldn't answer.

"What's your Boss's name, Carl?"

That stumps me again. I don't think I've ever thought about it. While I'm trying to come up with an answer, she says "Where were you coming from, when they picked you up?"

"Um, I'd rather not say, Miss O'Hara."

Then she says, just as kind and sweet as you can imagine, "It's no big secret, Carl. You were in prison and it wasn't easy time for you. There's no shame in it. I just want to ask you one thing more. Do you remember when you got out?"

All the sudden the wind dies and that terrible Florida heat has me in a ratcheting headlock. I ache all over. The Boss's name, when I got out, why don't I remember these things? The sweat's pouring down my forehead, into my eyes, salty on my tongue.

She's got me so bollixed up I hardly notice that we're almost at the Slippery Slope. I only start to come out of it when I notice a little twisty movement out of the corner of my eye. Then another and another. I turn to look and there they are, one worm after another, wriggling out of the ground, then up, slowly up, right off into the air, like they were crawling right up the moonlight. Millions of them, nightcrawlers, little pinworms and great big prehistoric Florida swamp worms, swarming slowly into the sky, glistening wet in the golden light. At that rate it'll take them years to reach the moon, but they don't look like they're in any hurry.

I don't know how long I watch them, my mouth hanging open like a big ol' sucker fish, till I feel Sweet Selena's back tilt under me and realize that we're thirty feet up the Slippery Slope and I got to do something. I slide off to one side and land on my butt. "Lady," I say when I catch my breath, "who are you and what the Hell's happening here?"

She smiles, wreathed in dreads that glow in the moonlight, from atop that white mare and it's hard to look at her. Not the kind of shaky bowel feel you get when you don't want to look anywhere near the Boss, or the chill down your spine when Werther-Bob's too close. It's something so sweet you're afraid you'll start bawling and never stop.

"Carl," she says, "what is it every Groom needs?"

"Umm, a hoof pick?"

She smiles and shakes her head.

"A curry comb?"

"No, Carl. A Bride."

Of all the crazy things people've been saying to me, this takes the cake. "You're my Wife?" I know I forget things, but this?

Becky laughs, not a prom queen titter, but a big, hearty guffaw that's still pretty as a wind chime. It sounds so nice I'm not even embarrassed. She could laugh at me all day long like that.

"Let's just say I'm the Maid of Honor."

That makes as much sense as everything else, which is none.

"You didn't answer my question. What's going on here?"

"That would take a long time to explain."

"Try it before I up and look for Biscayne on my own." I say, trying to sound a lot tougher than I'm feeling.

"OK." She points back at the fair ground. "What do you see there, Carl?"

"The show. Buncha stables and horses."

"But not just any horses, but the world's best, most expensive ones, here because it's where the rich send their prize hunters and jumpers in winter. And surrounding them, all the riders, trainers, security, grooms like you. Billions of dollars tied up in this, all to see some pretty horses do a few tricks. Money that could go to feed people, teach them, clothe them, all here because that's not what a few rich Owners want."

"No offence, ma'am, but are you some kind of communist?"

That golden laugh again. "Not exactly. Carl, what do you think money is?"

I don't care how pretty she is. I've had about enough of this crap. How come nobody ever talks straight around here? "Money is money, is all."

"Money is stored energy. And when you put all that dammed up energy together in the same place, year after year, it creates a pattern, a kind of stable vortex that sucks things in and attunes other energies to itself. Things get lost in it. People too," she says quietly, laying a hand on my shoulder. "Whirling around endlessly, broken to pieces, with no place to go but down, eventually. That's what Hell is, Carl."

I'm starting to get a sick feeling in the pit of my stomach. "That's crazy talk. It's just a show. It's on for a few days and you get run off your feet, but then it's over. Everybody goes home."

"You're right, Carl," Becky says gently. "Some people do. When's the last time you went home?" When I don't say anything, she asks, "Do you remember it?"

Of course I do, I think. But when I actually try to remember the last time I went home, anytime I went home, home at all, I come up with a vague jumble of faces I can't see well, places I half remember, voices I never listened to. I'm starting to sweat again and not from the heat. My ribs hurt. I feel sick.

"You were an orphan, raised in a string of foster homes," she says in that terrible gentle way she has and I know it's true. "People like you are vulnerable, Carl. You've got so little to anchor you to the world."

"But why are you all talking to me? I'm no one special, you said so yourself. How come you and Werther-Bob and the Boss are on my case right now?"

"Have you ever heard of the Butterfly Effect, Carl?"

I just shake my head.

"It's the idea that a tiny change, the flutter of a butterfly wing, can change things enough to bring on a great storm."

"That don't make sense. Werther-Bob says--"

"The talking dog?"

"Well, yeah... he says--"

"He says you're a pissant and you'll never change anything, right?" She hears the yes in my silence. "I wonder why he has to keep telling you that, Carl. Maybe he knows, like I know, that there's something about you and Biscayne, something powerful, and he has to stop it."

"Lady, all I do is clean hooves and muck out stables. There's hundreds of horses and grooms here, plus a lot of people with more clout than I'll ever have. Why me and that particular horse?"

"No one knows, Carl. We just feel it."

"But--"

Just then there's a shrill neigh and I look back to see Biscayne at the bottom of the Slippery Slope. He's breathing heavy, mouth chomping and that dong halfway to the ground. He paws the ground, glaring up at us, crazy and bloodshot. It finally hits me--the tail flicks and dancing around--Sweet Selena's the mare in heat.

Becky says quietly, "Jump up here with me, Carl. We're riding out of here." What in Hell is this girl trying to get me into?

A flash of black in the corner of my eye and Werther-Bob's halfway up the slope, snarling. He leaps and he's on Becky, knocking her sideways off Sweet Selena. The mare screams and wheels, kicking out. Both hooves catch Werther-Bob square and he goes flying, ass over teakettle. I'm trying to see how bad Becky's hurt when I feel the rock of slope drumming under me and look up just in time to roll out of Biscayne's way.

I can't see Becky. Somehow it's gotten really bright, like the moon's turned into a searchlight. There's something I almost remember, something I need to remember. Where's Becky? Then the rock drums again and Sweet Selena is thundering down on me. She's too fast and too close...

And hurdles me like a low hedge, with Biscayne leaping right behind her, landing where she was a split second before. It's a crazy steeplechase under the blazing moon...

Then Biscayne loses his footing, just as he's about to catch up with Selena. He screams as his foreleg buckles, then lurches into her and both of them tumble, over and over, down the Slippery Slope, shrieking and neighing in terror and pain.

They hit the level ground tangled up together. It's still and quiet, for a few seconds. Then Selena gets her legs under her, shakily.

Miraculously she doesn't seem to be hurt badly, though there's a gash on her left flank. She nuzzles Biscayne, then startles and bolts when he screams and bites her.

Biscayne heaves himself up. It takes him three tries. All I can do is watch. It's like I'm paralyzed. There's something wrong with his back. His right back hoof drags. But he's still erect and he brays a challenge before limping off after Sweet Selena. In seconds they're both out of sight on a path through a thicket of cottonwoods and black locust. I can hear their hoofbeats, hers trotting, his stumbling, fading away.

"Well, Bubba, looks like you're really in the shit now." Werther-Bob's voice is faint. It hurts to look at the way his body's twisted.

I don't answer him and turn away. Where's Becky? Why can't I see her?

"She ain't here," the thing in a dog's shape says. "Riders always just up and go. Guys like us, we stay and shovel the shit that's left behind."

"Fuck you, you God damned... what the hell are you anyway? What have you done with Becky?"

"Carl, I b'lieve you're finally startin' to wake up. Bout time, too." Incredibly, he starts to clamber to his feet. He falls, twice, but makes it up. "I tol' you, she's gone. Forget her. You got other things to do. Now go tell the Boss what's happened here."

"The Boss and you can kiss my ass." I'm trying to sound a lot braver than I feel. Even crippled, Werther-Bob scares me bad.

"Wrong answer, Bubba. You made an agreement. It ain't a matter of what you wanna do." He takes a step, then another. He only seems able to move sideways. There's something wrong with his hip. He loses his footing and falls with a groan.

"Yeah? We'll see about that." I get up. My backside hurts a bit from where I fell off Sweet Selena, but otherwise I'm OK. I clamber carefully down the Slippery Slope, giving Werther-Bob a wide berth. "I'm tired of your bullshit. Nobody tells me anything around here. I'm going to find Becky and that's the last you'll see of me." There's a whirling, whistling sound off to my left and I suddenly realize there's a tornado somewhere close.

I hear another shaky, hissing off to my side and turn to see Werther-Bob, still on the ground, convulsed with laughter. He's laughing so hard he can't even concentrate on getting up. It sounds about as bad you'd expect a laughing, crippled demon Doberman to sound.

"Bubba, we been tryin' to tell you what's what since you got here. You jes' ain't been up to listening." He sobers up. Some weird, carnivore mutation of compassion passes over his face. "You want answers, Carl, you got to talk to the Boss. Guaranteed you won't like what you hear, but he'll tell you the truth." He starts trying to get up again and I decide it's high time I made tracks.

I'm halfway through a stand of thorny locust, dodging branches whipping and moaning in the wind, trying to keep to from getting scratched up too bad when someone taps my shoulder.

I whirl. Nobody there. I'm spooked as it is, snapping my head back and forth, glaring into the shadows. The groan that comes from the locust bush almost jolts me out of my skin. I peer closer.

It's Huong. Somehow he's got himself rammed back into the thick of the branches. Even in the dim light I can see he doesn't look good, his shirt torn, skin raked and bloody with thorns. His feet don't seem to be touching the ground.

"Jesus, Huong, what happened to you?"

He shakes his head impatiently, as if it didn't matter. His right eye's almost swollen shut. "Got kicked. You see Biscayne?" I can hardly hear him over the wind.

"Saw him and lost him again. We got to get you out of there, buddy."

He sucks in a breath and I hear something gurgle inside. "Can't." I'm about to say something when the moon comes clear of a cloud and the wind shifts, giving me a clear view of him. The big branch I thought was under his armpit has punched through his chest, a few long thorns still on it, dripping dark blood.

"Oh Christ, Huong."

"Never mind. You find Biscayne. Take this." He starts hauling on something tangled in the locust withes, wincing with effort.

"Fuck, Huong, stay still. Just stay still until I can get some help."

"No time. I don't last that long. You find Biscayne. Run."

And I'm about to, when I think to ask "Did you see a blonde girl or a white mare? Sweet Selena?"

"There is Rider?"

"A Rider, sure, yeah. You seen her?"

"No, I don't see her." He frowns, mouth working. "You go to Boss. He tell you."

"What the hell is the Boss going to tell me that I don't know? Werther-Bob's crippled, fit to die. You're about dead already. There's a tornado coming, Becky's riding a mare in heat and getting chased by Biscayne, who's liable to kill her if he don't kill himself first. I got to get there before he does."

"You see her soon. First take this." Huong's finally got whatever he's been yanking at free. He thrusts it through the spiky tangle by main force. It's one of the bridles he's been polishing. In the moonlight it glows like a knot of dark ribbon. It feels warm and alive as I take it out of his big hand.

"Huong, I'll never get this on him without help, unless he's dead when I get to him. And everybody'll be too busy loading up horses and getting out of there. I got to find Becky."

"First you find Boss. He tell you what to do. Then you see Rider."

"All of the sudden you're sounding like Werther-Bob. What gives?"

"Dog and me want different things. But we both know same thing happen now. Must pay respects."

"But--"

He grits out "You do what I could not. Go now."

I'm about to, when I think of something. "Hey, Huong."

He slowly opens his left eye.

"I saw them. The worms, crawling up into the sky."

He smiles and that's the last time he moves.

For a while I just stand there, wanting to do something, wanting to be anywhere else but here, but unable to move. Then I hear a horse scream towards the fairgrounds and I know I've got to go.

It's crazy when I get back, wild-eyed horses shying this way and that, chased by grooms and riders, hauled, balking and rearing into stall trailers and semis, drivers honking, cursing and cutting each other off. Over the moon there's an scab-ugly black cloud, edges lit up by lightning and the wind shrieks like a whipped cat. There's no funnel yet, but everyone knows it's coming.

I can't see Becky, Sweet Selena or Biscayne anywhere. Somehow, no matter which way I go, I always seem to end up at the End Times Poker tent. It seems to be the only thing that's not affected by the storm, gray canvas swaying gently, as if by gentle breezes. Pedro stalks around the entrance, muttering and singing and talking to whoever it is he sees in the dust on his brain. He's got his knife out, but he doesn't seem to notice me, even though I all but fall over him once, following a horse I thought was Biscayne. Finally, I'm so tired I just surrender, draw back the flaps and walk in.

It's dark there, lit only by one old-fashioned oil lamp, swaying gently back and forth. It's a big tent, but it seems like it's full of people, hovering back in the shadows. In fact the only thing I can really see clearly is a big round table, covered with green baize. Somebody's just finished dealing the flop on a game of seven card stud. Outside horses are neighing and whinnying, riders and grooms shouting, engines grinding, but here it's quiet. Someone says "Pair of queens leads," and the bets go round the table.

"Nice to see you again, Carl." It's a voice like fine dirt sifting into an open grave.

I guess this'd be the Boss. I don't know, maybe I just never looked at him closely before. What I see is a little olive-skinned guy with a full head of white hair combed up to a big pompadour. He's got piercing, close-set eyes over a big beaky schnozz. In all the heat and humidity he's wearing pin-striped three-piece suit. He leans close and I can smell his cologne and the fat black cigar he's smoking.

He nods to the dealer. "Fold. Deal me out for a while." Then he turns and those black eyes have me pinned in place. "Are you going to find my stallion, Carl?"

"Yes sir, it's just that...

"What?"

And it just comes spilling out of me, Werther-Bob, Becky, the Slippery Slope, Biscayne getting hurt, the worms, Huong... I don't so much end as dribble to a stop. I look at the Boss and it seems like I've asked more questions than I've answered.

The Boss looks down at his big folded hands. He doesn't seem too upset with the news about Biscayne, even though I've seen horses put down with injuries less serious. He sighs. "You'd like some answers, wouldn't you?" and I suddenly feel like we've done this before. I nod.

"Everything that... girl, that Rider said to you was true, more or less."

"So this is Hell?"

He glances to one side and I suddenly realize there are bigger fish than the Boss around, things that scare him as much as he scares me. It's not an idea I want to explore. "Let's just say the Show creates its own order. It brings together places and things most people believe are separate, keeps things going long past what you'd normally call their due date."

"I can't remember things. Am I dreaming? Am I dead?"

He gets up from the table and stretches. His arms are really long for a short guy. I suddenly remember a condor I saw in a zoo when I was a kid, how desolate and crazy it looked, penned up with the sky forever out of reach. He lays a heavy hand on my shoulder and it's icy through my t-shirt.

"Somewhere you're lying in a prison yard with a rat-tail shank stuck in your heart. Somewhere you're buried in a potters field. Here, though..." He's walking me to the tent flap, herding me, really.

"Here, what?"

"Here what I need to tell you is you've got a job to do. Find Biscayne. Because if he goes..." He's opening the flap.

"Why is that my job? Why's everyone talking to me all of a sudden? Why does Werther-Bob hate Huong? What are they? Why--"

"Too many questions for now. Just find that horse and bring him back."

Then something comes over me I can't explain. I get the feeling, no, I can remember him telling me this thousands of times. Except it's different people, not exactly me and not precisely him. Sometimes I'm looking up at him and sometimes down. He's dressed in all different clothes, some like things you see in history movies, some I can't even describe. But he always tells me what to do and I do it.

So I stop. Even though my head's aching and my body's paining me bad, telling me to run, get out of that tent, find Biscayne and be done with it, I stop. I can't even tell him I'm not doing what he says. My mouth's too dry and it won't make those words. I just plant my feet and stare back at him. If it kills me, I ain't gonna move till he tells me why.

And Lord help me, he stops too. The big hand falls off my shoulder and he takes a good look at me, like a buzzard before it hops over to a carcass. Something like a smile crosses his face, but it's gone almost before I notice. He puffs his cigar, then says "You're not moving till I tell you what's happening. Is that it, Carl?"

Crawling to the Moon, Page 21

My head feels like a boulder on my shoulders, but I manage to nod.

"Can it wait just a moment? I need some air."

I nod again and he opens the tent flap. You'd think he'd need both hands lifting the heavy canvas against the wind, but that big hand pushes it out like the sash of a silken pavilion on a calm spring morning and holds it open with no strain. We stand there looking out.

It's even crazier than before. A couple of tractor trailers have pitched over. I can hear horses screaming and kicking inside. The wind is grabbing big hunks of sod and sailing them like frisbees. Some fool's shooting at whatever moves. I see all these things, but it's like it's at a distance, below me somehow. I wonder idly if Owners always feel like this.

"Everybody's so sure the world will go on, the sun will rise tomorrow and they'll have a second chance." The Boss stops and lights another big black cigar. Maybe I'm not seeing right, but he seems to do it without a match or lighter. "But you can see for yourself, things go smash if everyone doesn't do their jobs."

"But--"

"Why you? It wasn't always you. Before that it was Huong. And before him, Pedro. Or the other way around. I forget things, Carl, just like you. I think, a long time ago, it was me. We did our job and the world goes on the only way it's got to go on. It isn't pretty sometimes and drives some people crazy." He gestures with his cigar and I see Pedro, knife waving wildly, chasing a little girl on a pony. "Maybe that Rider's got you thinking you can get out. There isn't any out. There's the Show," he nods toward the tent, "and there's Chaos. And that's all there is."

He's got the black cigar lit and he's holding it out. For me. The world has gotten very quiet. The game has stopped, I realize. I see the rich, gray smoke coming off the cigar in little dancing spirals. I see the look in The Boss's eyes, lost and empty above his gloating smirk. I reach for the cigar...

Just then a faint scream floats to me from a long way off. I can't tell if it's a horse, a woman or a man. I look at The Boss, at the shadows huddled inside the End Times Poker Tent, at the ruination outside. And I slap that cigar to the ground.

Crawling to the Moon, Page 22

The Boss's mouth hangs open and it's like I can see right into him, only there ain't nothing to see. He's just a man-shaped space in a pin-striped suit. A sudden hard gust rips the canvas out of his hand and The Boss lurches against me. His mouth is at my ear. "I'm tired, Carl," he whispers. "We're all so tired." The oil light flares up and for a moment I can see all the way into the tent. They're gathered there, held together by silk suits and evening gowns, rags of flesh falling off their bones, skulls so weary they've lost their grins, all looking back at me, cards slack in skeletal fingers. Only the dealer moves, his back to me, shuffling the cards again. Then the flap bangs shut and I'm outside.

And out there the twister's finally leaped out of the storm. The air's full of screaming from people, horses and wind. Through dirt and rain you can only see it sometimes, hopscotching across the road, plucking the asphalt like a finger pulling a bass string. While I watch it snatches up a semi-trailer and plays crack-the-whip, spilling truck wheels and shrieking horses.

Then it splits into countless little dust devils. Up ahead of me there's a glittering whirl and I can see it's horseshoes, shredded credit cards and rain, sparking and clattering, caught in a fierce little eddy. Below it I swear the earth itself is churning. As I watch, the dust devil slams into another, then another and the tornado's back again. It sidles my way and I know it's time to leave.

I really can't say how long I run, dodging rocks, branches and pieces of the Show hurled by howling winds. I'm frantically looking for a ditch, a hole, anywhere low where I can take cover when I trip over a horse.

It's Biscayne. He's alive, barely, and the madness has left him. He nickers gently and nuzzles my hand. Somehow the sight of him, still golden and beautiful lying broken in the red Florida muck, strikes me as the worst thing I've ever seen. I weep then, forgetting where I am, cradling and stroking the big tawny head. He sniffs around my pockets, looking for a treat. He knocks loose the bridle Huong gave me, which all the time I'd forgotten was on my shoulder. For some reason I slip it over his head. He doesn't resist, just sighs and closes his eyes.

It's quiet then. The wind stops squalling, like a baby finally back at its mother's breast. I look around and the sun's first rays glow through the edges of the black cloud. Gently laying Biscayne's head down, I gradually get to my feet, straddling his golden neck, stretching and sighing.

--then blinded and deafened by the lightning bolt that blasts the grass into flame not ten feet away. When the red fades a bit I can see the flames stalking closer, but I barely notice. Above me the twister looms black as God's horsewhip, now swaying ponderously, now leaping around and above me, hemming me in, paralyzing me, a tiny crawling thing at the foot of a giant. I can feel its roaring in my spine.

I'm heaved up, not by the clutching wind, but from below. I look down and there's Biscayne, stumbling to his feet, hoisting me up with him. He trembles and I nearly slide off, just managing to catch myself by snatching at the bridle. I think I must be hurting him but he hardly seems to notice me. He neighs a challenge and I look up. Up above there's a light, almost too bright to look at. I think it looks like a girl on a horse but maybe I'm crazy and it's just the moon.

Biscayne stumbles, screaming in pain and I think I should get off. While I'm trying to balance so I don't hurt him when I step down I see the tornado race back and plunge into the End Times Poker Game tent, ripping up stakes and sending it wheeling and darting like an enormous bat, scattering cold gray dust. Everything seems to sizzle briefly, as if what had been a standing wave till then suddenly moved through and beyond. I can see the showgrounds, covered with splintered stalls, straw and dust, men and horses rushing back and forth. I can see something dog-shaped and black racing towards us sideways and a gleam of white teeth. Before I can dismount Biscayne rears with his last strength. The light is still above us. I don't know what it looks like now. What I can feel is Biscayne's hooves somehow finding purchase in the cold dark wind. We're going up. I—

Comment

This one grew out of one of many jobs I wasn't very good at, being a groom on the Florida horse show circuit circa 1974, a wild and exhausting few months. In my late teens I worked for a few months on a boarding ranch and then on the horse show circuit in Florida, which then, as now, was a place for America to get its weird on. The shows, Ocala, Orlando and Jacksonville, were simultaneously miracles of long-term planning, on-the-spot muscle and cooperation, and sheer, bat-shit craziness, to a degree that's impossible to overstate.

Think of rural central and northern Florida, home of militias, walking catfish, car-swallowing sinkholes and poison oak, suddenly descended on by American plutocrats, Eurotrash jet-setters, Saudi and Gulf Emirate royalty and all their layers of security and courtiers. Add in handlers, managers and especially riders, obsessive, often anorexic, coke-snorting peak athletes, both imperious to underlings and totally at the beck and call of whatever magnate or mafioso paid their bills. Then grooms, of whom I was one, the serfs, up at four to braid manes and tails, then mucking out stalls, tacking up and tacking down, cleaning hooves, rubbing, wrapping, watering and feeding till dark, when you'd grab a bite, a few hours of sleep, and usually be waked up around midnight because some of your charges had escaped their cheaply built, temporary stalls. And finally the stars of all this: The horses, hunters and jumpers, mostly ex-racehorses with a sprinkling of Barbs, Quarter Horses, and even Percheron crosses thrown in, most of them essentially beautiful, finely tuned tax shelters on the hoof, animate conversation pieces and gambling tokens for the Beautiful People, which is to say stars, emirs, entrepreneurs, trust-fund kids and scum.

All of these came together for three weeks on the Florida winter circuit, a movable feast of horse-trading (literally), jockeying (pun inescapable) for prestige and insanity, fueled by too much money and too many drugs, including PCP, which, as horse tranquilizer, could be had just about anywhere.

So trust me when I tell you that, while this story's events are fantastic, the setting is just what you'd expect of a regular day on the Circuit, ca 1974, and possibly even now.

Interestingly, one of the details people in my writers group had the most trouble believing was completely true: At that time, the horses were housed in extremely flimsy stalls that were only made to last for a few days. So you'd get up in the early morning to braid manes, water and feed the horses, run around like a madman all day tacking and untacking them, delivering and taking them back from events, rubbing them down in the evening, snatch a supper and go to sleep around 10. Then get waked up around midnight, because some of your zillion dollar horses had leaned up against their ticky-tack stalls, stumbled through and were now wandering around, through poison oak and palmetto scrub, like stoned sleepwalkers.

The End

MONSOON

And when the rains come she is back again, back between the horns of Rama, our buffalo, as Parameswaran, my husband's youngest, leads him in from the paddy. Only a little mist, you could miss her if you didn't watch.

They say I don't know, I'm not from this village. My mother-in-law, bending over the kerosene burner, tells me to hold my tongue.

A little dal missing from the pot each day.

Jag, my husband groans in his sleep, muttering in the river dialect. Sometimes sip of cha, gone from the teapot, a low chuckle I can never locate. I want to go home, but they have spent my dowry.

They say I am barren, but Jag will not lie with me. He says he is too tired, but he stalks through the compound at night, from the gate to the barn and between the huts. And the rain, always the rain.

She moves, I can hear her, her pattering feet and the kerosene stove hissing in her damp, in the next hut where my mother-in-law sleeps and the rattan sags a little more into the red mud.

In the next village, they rounded up everyone for cholera vaccinations, old men, babies screaming with fear. The soldiers lined them up and the doctor stabbed them with his needle. Now they have hepatitis. I know this word: My father gave me books. Better he should have given me a larger dowry.

Across our walled compound, I can hear her at night, talking to Jag, her liquid whispers, laughing at his "fine, educated wife".

The rain comes down harder and she dances, the gold in her bangles ringing as she sidles and stamps, the thatch of our roof rustling and sighing with her movements. I can hear my mother-in-law snoring, sleeping near the kerosene stove.

I'm going over there.

This has to stop.

The End

Crawling to the Moon, Page 27

SYSTEMS CRASH

"Another beer, Frank?"

"Thanks, Hal. Yeah, set me up again."

"So, what's happening?"

"Saw Estelle at a party a while back."

"Oh man, when are you going to get over that chick? Lookit, Frank, she's no good for you. She's good-looking, she's sexy, she's bright enough, I guess. But she's the Queen of the Bitches. Look at how she dumped you. Everybody says so."

"Hey, chill. I just said I saw her. Well, actually, I knew she'd be there."

"Why am I not surprised?"

"Yeah, she was with her new boyfriend, Jerry Martens."

"Jerry Martens? That prick whose Dad ran the chemical plant? The one who always used to sneer at us when we did the pizza delivery to his parties?"

"Yeah, rich Jerry. His Daddy died and he cleaned up on the will. He's finishing up his Master's in Business. Got himself chopped, cloned and networked."

"Heavy gold."

"You're not kidding. Dude must have towed in five mil in parts. Fast-twitch grafts, great hair, cheekbones you could cut yourself on, bone extension so he's damn near seven feet tall, mylar contacts, the whole nine yards. He had on one of those fastpeek jumpsuits, with random transparencies so's you could scope out his manly fizzicue. Hung like a Triple Crown winner, now, too."

"Subtle."

"Well, that's Estelle and Jerry: Always go with class. He's even got four little ornamental aerials on his left temple, so you know that somewhere he's got four dedicated clones doing the mental gruntwork, making him look good. Just in case you miss the point. I take one look at him and think 'No way am I tangling with that, all on my lonesome.'"

"Now you're finally talking sense."

"But he starts in, needling me 'bout my job and him going to Dartmouth, with Estelle laughing and egging him on and I figure what the hell, so we start arguing."

"About what?"

"Kind of a question is that? These things are never 'about' anything, they're just dicksize wars and he's got me beat seven ways to Sunday."

"Oh, I don't like the sound of this..."

"Yeah, Jerry's talking rings, no, talking Dyson Spheres around me. You want facts and figures? He's got 'em, pipin' hot out of the databank. He's even wired up with one of those little Toshiba handholos, so he can do 3-D graphs, right in your face. You want literary? He's got epigrams from Moliere, Sappho, Oscar Wilde, the Gilgamesh cycle, Kristeva, George Sand, I mean it's all coming at me, so fast and funny and furious all I can do is gape. I remember some of the stuff he said and now it don't mean much of anything, but at the time he sounds like a genius. The guy's in the zone, he's smoking a Davidoff Double Corona and drinking a Tidepool, with the kava, vodka and the live crab? The fuck does he care, he's got neural cutouts, he can do that shit all night long. Smiling his great smile that cost more money 'n I make in a year. Everyone's watching this post-human dirtbag access his four little flunkies to flatten my butt while Estelle giggles and wiggles like a cat in heat. Everything's going according to schedule."

"Bad scene."

"So meanwhile, Roberta and Cherysse... "

"Wait a minute. Roberta and Cherysse were there? Man, what the hell are you still sniffin' around Estelle for? Roberta's twice as smart, easy to look at and she actually likes you, Christ knows why."

"Yeah, I know. We been out a few times."

"And Cherysse! Whoa-ho-ooh-whee! That girl is a jaw-dropper."

"Down boy. And they're not there."

"But you just said - "

"Will you let me tell it?"

"Sec. I gotta get some customers. Two Becks and a Gimlet? Comin' up."

* * *

"So?"

"So, meanwhile, Roberta and Cherysse are out in Silverwood, talkin' to these security guys at one of those secure condos?"

"Is this where... "

"Right. Where the clones are stashed. Little utility apartment down in the basement."

"How'd you find it?"

"Some hacking and cracking on my part and Roberta's. That girl can pull code apart like you untie your shoelaces. Cherysse helped with social engineering."

"I can just guess. And what are they getting out of this?"

"Well, Roberta never did like Estelle much. Calls her a parasite. Plus, she says this is going to be part of her research project."

"If Roberta ever puts whatever that is all together, the world's in for a shock."

"And Cherysse, besides being Roberta's bud, had her own little run-in with Jerry a while back. It got kind of ugly."

"OK, they're there. Now what?"

"Well, they're with the security guys and everybody's relaxed. Couple good-lookin' girls, Friday night, talkin' that sweet trash and with their own tokes. Hey, everybody's gotta loosen up sometime, am I right?"

"Ahh..."

"Yeah, just a light trank in the weed, just enough to leave Joberto and Otis in dreamland, there in the employees' lounge."

"So they're in. What now? Go knock out the clones? Take down the link?"

"Please. Leave us not be crude. No, they go knock on the door and one of these guys answers. A Jerry. Except he's not like our hero, currently hanging me out to dry, ten miles away in midtown. No, he's pudgy and shy and awkward and kind of near-sighted. And he's got all the social graces and confidence of a zit-faced fourteen-year-old whose voice is cracking and who can't help getting boners in public."

"A nerd."

Crawling to the Moon, Page 31

"Of the first water. They're all of them nerds, sitting there at their consoles, looking through databanks, one or the other miming out Jerry One's party talk. Oh, one's had most of the implants and grafts, just in case Jerry One needs a backup, but basically they never get out, they don't talk to anybody, they don't know from anything except getting Number One the answers and grades, while he's off living the high life."

"But aren't they suspicious?"

"Roberta's a pretty good talker. And Cherysse, well, suspicion is kind of beside the point, when she sets out to charm guys about as sophisticated as Butthead's little brother."

"So what happens?"

"What happens is Roberta gives them a survey."

"A survey?"

"We cobbled one together, out of some I found in a dumpster. A long survey, with questions that meander all over the place and that you have to think about for a long time to make sure you're giving exactly the answer you really want to give. It's about politics, lifestyles, their spiritual thoughts, their toothpaste purchasing habits. And they love it. No one's ever asked them what they think about anything before."

"So, meanwhile... "

"Jerry's losing his edge. No one notices but me, but his eyes are wandering, like he's having trouble concentrating. I come on a little stronger and start pressing him for stock tips. That gets his attention - he can handle that stuff on his own - and he starts bragging about the killing he made on the floor this morning. Then they get to page eight."

"Page eight?"

"Page eight is where the survey goes off in different directions. Jerry Two gets questions on his sexual preferences, Three a bunch of Libertarian propaganda, Four has to think about where he'd like to vacation and gamble, Five does a long questionnaire on crop herbicides. And guess what? While the four Jerries are distracted, Roberta's toggled their com-board so Jerry One, uptown, is getting all their responses, all at once. And he can't turn it off without doing something really drastic to the receiver at the base of his jaw."

"How'd this play back at the party?"

"Jerry 1 definitely looks a little flustered. He keeps blurting things about Posse Comitatus, anal sex, Roundup and Atlantic City. Estelle tries to get him to leave. I make fun of his clothes. And hers, while I'm at it."

"I'm sorry I missed it."

"Meanwhile, back at the ranch, Cherysse peels off her outfit. Underneath she's got on about as skimpy a bodysuit as anyone can stick on a body like hers. She puts on a dance disc, a really fast one with a cumbia beat and gets them all jazzercising, as much as they can while they watch her bounce and stretch. All this while Roberta barks weird questions at them."

"Oh, man."

"Yeah, Jerry's jerking and twitching, trying to do a merengue and crunchies and recite the Bhagavad Gita at the same time. By this time, everybody's figured out what's happening and they're all laughing and clapping in time. Plus, it turns out Estelle and he are wired up so they're always in synch when they're dancing. Well, somehow that circuit cuts in, so they're doing this stuff in unison."

"Jeez, this is great!"

"All of the sudden, Jerry freezes. Total systems crash. Falls down on the couch, knocks over his drink. The crab gets out and pinches him on the nose."

"So, is he OK?"

"They're bringing him around slowly. Right now, he can count to a hundred and he likes to play Go Fish. They figure he'll make full recovery, but it'll take time. They're not sure if he can ever link up again. The quadruplets are fine, never better. They were in Disney World, last I heard, having a ball. The estate pays for it all."

"And Estelle?"

"Someone told me she was waiting tables at Maloney's, just off the Interstate. Could I get another beer?"

The End

FISHING FOR POMOS

So I'm getting ready to leave the job interview and I notice a big angling trophy, a muskellunge, on the wall.

Thinking "Here's a chance to butter the guy up in a hale-fellow-well-met way," I say, admiringly, "That's quite a lunker."

"Caught him up at Black Lake. He's all plastic."

"Oh." (trying to sound knowledgeable) "Boy, the things they can do now. Just the soak the sucker in quick-drying epoxy, I guess, and - "

"No, no, they just measure the length and girth. Then you eat your fish or throw him away - whatever. Couple weeks later, you got your lunker in the mail. Looks better than the one you caught. And it's the right size, too and easier to wall mount, 'cause it's light."

"Well, that's convenient."

"See that pattern on his belly? Every lake, the fish have different markings. You don't even have to pay extra. Part of the service."

"I'll have to get the business card from you, sometime. Well, I guess I'll be - "

"It's a real growth industry. I bought in quick. They're going public next month. And expanding into new lines."

"Man, I'll have to have my broker check that out. Anyway, it's been - "

"Brings a whole, new dimension to the words 'Trophy Wife.'"

The End

BHARIA

"Take me up," the dead Queen said, "up and into the light. I must light the fire."

The voice, dry as a bone rattle, shook Aeoma from a waking dream of moonlight, drums and flame, of being led by this same voice, pulling her like a rope. Her head spun and she fell back against a limestone wall, rough and damp against her back. She gagged as her nostrils filled with the stench of rotting flesh. What witchery had brought her here, against all the teachings, alone and unpurified, to the Cave of Souls? Far above the girl could hear the faint bray of rams' horns and conches, the pounding rush of drums and dancing feet. But here the air was still and heavy with the sweet reek of death.

Turning her head slowly, in the dim torchlight she saw she was five paces from the rope ladder. She couldn't tell whether the Guardian Stone blocked the hole and she was afraid to look more closely. Had anyone missed her? She had vague flashes of memory: wild-eyed celebrants hurling themselves into the frenzied dance, heedless of a small girl threading her way among them to the Pit of the Dead. Whatever it was that spoke with the Queen's voice, it was powerful to draw her here, unwitting and unbeknownst to the People gathered above.

"Take me up, sister-daughter," the thing whined. It sprawled back on the throne, gowned in gold embroidered linen, decked in rare feathers and onyx beads, an ermine cape draped loosely over thin shoulders, a soapstone carving of the Fat Mother on its lap. Aeoma remembered when the Queen was a human image of the little figurine, shoulders hung with massive, pendulous breasts and great, fertile hips straining her dress. Bharia had caught the wasting sickness, but how had she become this thin? This must be a demon to work so quickly in the three days since death, she decided.

"Above is the meagre abode of the living," she said, struggling to keep her 11 year old voice steady, reasonable. "It's night and dark as here. The fires are lit for the Dance of the Dead Queen, in your honor." Aeoma answered from where she knelt before the Chair of the Great Dead, not daring to look at its occupant. "Down here," she gestured toward the hypogeum's walls, where painted herds grazed and frolicked, dim in the flicker of a single torch, "you have your cattle, sheep and goats, fatter and more hale than the scrawny herds of the island. You have your goods." As she edged toward the ladder, she pointed toward an array of household items ranged beside the corpse, a tortoiseshell comb, a fan of dark aromatic wood from Kush, a face paint box of Persian faience. "Finer than what is above, not lost or broken by careless hands, bleached in the sun or rotted in rain. You have the company of those you knew in life." A susurration grew from the ochre-soaked bones piled in the central pit, rising over the gnawing of beetles and maggots, flies buzzing and bat squeals. "Friends gone are with you always now. This is your true home, O Queen."

"Glib as ever," came the voice from the wasted body in the Chair, though its lips did not move. "I made no mistake in calling you, Aeoma. But you must take me up for our people's sake."

"Your people wish you only safe passage to the Land beyond the Western Mountains, so you may live with the Fat Mother and send us gentle spring rains, good crops, fine herds and full nets. That is what the true Queen, the Bharia that I knew and served, would want."

"Aeoma, how long has it been since the spring rains came in time for the people's corn? How long since they were the gentle rains of the old songs, not torrents drowning seed and fouling wells? I remember when a fisher could drag back his first cast, net full of wriggling silver, in sight of our shore. Can you? When last did the aurochs graze in long grass on the Dawn Plateau? Every year the mainlanders want more for a feast day bull, when they will sell them at all. This year Tyos and his drunken bravos had to steal one. The mainlanders may be weak, venal and divided, but they will only stand for so much. And do not sidle toward the ladder. I will be on you before you take two steps up."

"Tyos must have a bull for the funeral feast. You who call yourself Bharia know this is the teaching." Without warning, she screamed as loud as she could, reaching into her wool dress to pull out a necklace of beads from Harappa. In the centre was a teardrop-shaped piece of amber that she held in front of her, flickering as it caught the torchlight. The murmur of souls became a chorus of moans and snarls and she felt a tiny, cold breeze tickle her spine as the Dead cringed from a drop of the living Sun." When she drew a breath, the faint drumming and dancing above continued unabated. She began to chant a protection spell under her breath, using her free hand to salute the world's four quarters in turn.

"You remember your precautions, I see. Good, I taught you well. Better than my fool of a son."

Continuing to draw power from the Earth's quarters with her right hand, Aeoma spat out "Tyos is a faithful servant of the Fat Mother and no son of yours, demon."

"Demon, is it?" A desiccated chuckle hissed above the body. "Do you think I sent a dream to bring you down here, sister-daughter, so I could loiter beneath bridges or skulk around birth chairs? I could rule as Queen below with a fine carved head, while my son comes tomorrow to carry my skull in pomp and state to the Council Hall."

"I don't pretend to know the ways of the spirit world."

"Who knows them better? Not Tyos. He follows the teachings, but watches you to see what they mean and still does not understand. He's like a hunter who has been told where to track the boar but steps in its spoor without looking. He hates you for your talent and will kill you if he can."

"Now you use my own evil words to seduce me, demon."

"I use your own words because they are truths you spoke when I had others listening to what my people said." The voice softened. "Aeoma, if I am but a scheming, ravenous demon and not Bharia, your Bharia, then approach me with your drop of Sun between us." The girl hesitated, loath to approach the body in the Chair of the Great Dead. "Do it, girl, or the drumming will end and you'll be discovered. Or perhaps you will tire and I will eat you." It chuckled again.

Never taking her eyes off the dead Queen, Aeoma slipped the necklace off, holding it bunched in front of her so the amber teardrop was an arm's length between her and the demon. She took a

Crawling to the Moon, Page 39

shaky step, then another. The body didn't move and the dead eyes still looked at nothing.

"Good. Now place it on my breast," the bodiless voice commanded. The girl wavered. "If I am a demon it will scorch me. If I reach for you, push hard and your Sunstone will burn through to my heart. You know these things, little priestess."

Gathering all her nerve, Aeoma leaned over and gingerly touched the amber to the cold skin at the gown's neckline. There was an immediate flare of heat and she felt the dead flesh twitch. She leaped back, pulling the necklace, but it was stuck somehow, falling partway into the gown, so the beads trailed out of the round neckline. She caught a whiff of smoke through the miasma of death.

"How now, demon!"

She was halfway up the rope ladder when the dry voice stopped her. "Aeoma, are you strong enough to lift the Guardian Stone?"

She looked above and there was the frowning ogre face of the great capstone above her, sealing her in. "Come down, child," the dead Queen said reasonably. "We still have much to discuss, you and I."

Aeoma's only reply was to scuttle to the top of the ladder, huddling as near as she dared to the carved scowl of the Guardian Stone. She screamed again and again, then subsided to whimpering as the dead Queen sighed, then slowly got to her feet, tottering to the ladder. A thin stream of smoke rose steadily from the withered breast, but the thing seemed to pay it no mind, looping a shrivelled arm through a ladder rung and leaning heavily. "You disappoint me, sister-daughter. Ask yourself this: Why have I sent you a dream that brought you down here but no further, when I could have lured you within my grasp?"

"You toy with me, demon!"

"Aeoma, those the living call demons are nothing but souls without the luck or wit to find a home in the world. Like mindless flies they drift and flock, drawn by the scent of life. If they are evil, then so too are bees and mosquitoes." It sighed again, the dead eyes staring up into the shadows of the cave ceiling. "I have all time ahead of me. You and the People do not. Come down, please."

"Soon they will come and lift the Guardian Stone, thing. You can't climb and I will be free."

"Tell me how you will explain to my brilliant son Tyos how you lifted the Guardian Stone and what you did here, alone and unpurified. How long do you think you'll survive?"

There was a silence, filled only with the torch's crackling, the hiss and buzz of things feeding and far off chanting. Finally Aeoma gritted out "Stand away from the ladder."

"Gladly." Bharia staggered back to the Chair. Flopping down, she reached into her gown and yanked out Aeoma's bead necklace, tossing it to the stone floor, the amber bead still smoking. She nodded as the girl lunged and snatched it up.

"What do you want, Bharia?"

"Only what I asked for. Take me up and into the light. Dawn is coming."

"But why, my Queen? What is there for you in the lands above? If a teardrop of the Sun singes you, surely the Sun itself will set you ablaze. Why not stay down here, with your goods, your cattle and your friends, till the Fat Mother calls you beyond the Western Mountains?"

"Sister-daughter, as we speak the People are forming a line that stretches from the Cliff of the Great Cave all the way through the Temple Valley and into the Foggy Hills. Rich women bring masks of gold, shepherds their fattest rams, miners rings and bracelets carved from what onyx they can still find in the Southernmost Crags. Chieftains try to outdo each other with gifts of myrrh from across a distant desert, silks worth more than their tenants pay in tribute for a year. The poor, that is most in that line, hold thorn branches because their only gift is the blood they beat from their backs. All to pour in a hole in the ground, while the land turns to rock, the great forests of the east dwindle in memory and the People are poorer each day, save for the priests and the dead."

"What does it matter? Soon we will all be together with the Fat Mother in the land beyond the Western Mountains."

"Now you sound like my son. But I tell you, I have waited here two days and three nights. I, Bharia, a Queen strong in blood and magic, have waited while my drunken son and his priestling toadies have postured and eaten the fat of our land and the Fat Mother has shown herself not."

"What is three nights to an eternity with the Fat Mother in the blessed lands?"

"A good point, sister-daughter. Shall I tell that to King Tyrnios, who ruled when the Great Island was still green and shone with dew in the mornings? He's still here, though he doesn't remember much besides his name and that he is hungry. Shall I urge faith on shades of farmers and fishermen, from times before our first stories, who still mumble prayers to the Fat Mother, though they've forgotten their own names? Shall recommend patience to your mother, my dear sister Kabru, who watches you now as a hawk tracks a vole?"

"You lie. She is beyond--" A gesture from the Queen and a woman in linen robes appeared. Her hair was clumped and matted and her gaze blank and hungry as a pike. "Mother!" the girl cried and the thing snarled wordlessly, leaping and clawing towards her daughter even as it faded.

Then Aeoma wept, clawing her face, not caring where she was or what happened to her. "The dead do not rejoice, Aeoma," the dead Queen said gently, when the girl's sobs had quieted a little. "We don't want these things the People pour down here to honour and feed us, though they hold us in this place like a spider's web traps flies. We only desire what we cannot have, to live again. I let you burn me with your Sun's Tear because the pain was life to me, gave me the strength to move again. Even now though, I feel that strength and purpose ebbing, bleeding away into all the pious trash that fills this place."

The girl swallowed and was silent. She rose to her feet. "What must I do?" she asked, her voice steady.

"That's the brave Aeoma I remember. I need you to lend me your strength to crawl out of this burrow."

"You moved the Guardian Stone to bring me here. How is it you cannot shift yourself?"

"That is the difference between commanding others and mastering yourself. I am obeyed because of who I was and what I could do. But my body is weak with the sickness that killed me. Pull me up and let us go from this place."

"You will burn in the light!" But Aeoma held out her hand.

The Queen's grip was cold and fierce. Her lips moved with her voice for the first time. Her bodily voice was faint at first, but grew in strength. "Then I will burn like the dead of the Northmen who save their goods and strength for the living. When I was young I slew a mainland boar single-handed. I slaked my wanderlust from Harappa to the land of centaurs. I fought off invaders from Valya and the

Crawling to the Moon, Page 42

coughing plague from the east. I am Bharia, Queen of the Great Island and not a maggot, to gorge on carrion and hide from the sun. I will burn and they will sing of me for years to come."

She stood behind the girl, left hand on Aeoma's shoulder and flung her head back, eyes blazing at the Guardian Stone. In the dim light it seemed to Aeoma that the stone's carved scowl grew tighter and more fierce. "Aye, spirit in the rock, the hour is at hand," said Bharia. "Glare at us ever so dourly, you will do my bidding one last time. Now move aside, I command you." There was a silence, then slowly the great capstone began to roll out of the way, grinding its rocky haunches against the sides of the hole with the sound of a huge bear growling in his lair.

Immediately the flies' buzzing grew louder and more shrill. The hiss of feeding beetles and worms was like cold water splashed on a glowing hearthstone. "Hear me, sister-daughter. All the dead have is hunger for life, and their jealousy will stop us if you lose nerve. Take your beads in your mouth and keep the Sun's Tear clenched between your front teeth while we run the gauntlet of souls. Remember it is there and do not talk to them, whatever they may say. Do not look directly at them and keep moving. Ready?"

The girl nodded and stepped to the ladder. Suddenly the room grew quiet, as if everything were holding its breath. Even the drums from the ceremony above dimmed their pounding. Then Aeoma stepped on the first rope rung.

Through half-closed eyelids she saw the dead rise out of the pit of bones, out of the cave walls, from all the gifts left strewn about the hypogeum, like a gray mist gathering. She took another step up the ladder and they charged her like a flock of starlings swarms a tree, swooping at her face, clutching at her with almost substantial talons, shrieking faintly in her ears, gnashing ghostly teeth. She closed her eyes, bit down on the amber beginning to grow hot against her lips, and climbed up. Bharia's weight on her shoulder was scarcely heavier than carrying her little sister, but the dead Queen's clutch drew the heat out of her lungs, her heart. Aeoma shivered but kept going,

Abruptly the faint, horrid cacophony about her ceased and soft fingers stroked her cheek. Aeoma opened her eyes to see her mother, gazing at her tenderly. The girl gulped, her eyes stinging with tears. Kabru smiled softly and bent forward, her lips parted to kiss... A cold hand pushed her jaw shut and Aeoma realized she had nearly dropped the beads. "Do not look them, at any of them!" Bharia hissed. But before her eyes closed the girl saw the ghost's gaping jaws darting in, felt phantom teeth scraping faintly inside her.

And then they were through the hole and into the cave's upper chamber. The drumming and chanting were louder here and Aeoma caught a whiff of funerary incense. She could tell from the voices that the priests were getting ready to open the cave, to bring down the Last Gifts. Dawn must be close. The girl felt faint and the dead Queen's grip on her shoulder was like a cold blade next to her heart. "Let me go," Aeoma said.

The dead Queen seemed not to hear her. An ecstatic, idiotic grin wreathed Bharia's face as she gazed about her, already standing taller. "Let me go," Aeoma cried again. "You're hurting me!"

Bharia's dropped her hand and suddenly Aeoma could breathe again. There was a steady breeze and Aeoma filled her lungs with air that smelled only faintly of decay. The Queen turned away and when she turned back, her face was etched with compassion, something Aeoma realized she hadn't seen on that wilful visage for longer than she could remember. "I cannot weep, child, or I swear to the Fat Mother I would. Even now I am slipping, losing my mind and will. The pit calls to me and even the faint light here pains. Let us go while I still have strength, before I become another ravenous, mindless ghost."

Aeoma extended her hand, but Bharia shook her head. "Sister-daughter, you are the hope of the People of the Great Island now. All my deeds and boasts are not worth one breath in your throat. You are my Queen and my place is but to follow, if you will have me."

The girl stood silently, considering. "Should we not replace the Guardian Stone?" she said at last.

Bharia frowned. "Above the pit of souls I have no hold on him and my strength ebbs quickly. Let the bold among the dead rise up and blaze in the light if they would, is my counsel."

"Let it be, then."

They walked up the winding path, following the worn steps cut in the rock. When they came to a turning where a great figure of the Fat Mother was carved out of a huge green boulder, Aeoma made obeisance without thinking, chanting a prayer of praise to her breasts that fed the world. But Bharia stood silently, then nodded, saying "Maybe at last I will come to visit you now, All-Mother."

Crawling to the Moon, Page 44

As they walked the light grew stronger and the cave's ceiling was open to the sky gray sky in places where the thin stone had crumbled and fallen in. Bharia's steps began to lag and she skirted the patches of light.

Around another bend they came to a place just below the Door to the Underworld. Here the ceiling had fallen in completely and Aeoma could make out the words echoing down in the valley as Tyos stood unseen by the closed Door, chanting the Dead Feast Prayer, echoed by thousands of sleepless voices. Bharia stopped, then gathered herself and stepped into the soft twilight. A cloud shifted and sunbeam struck her as she was crossing. She screamed and leaped back to the shadows, gibbering. She started stumbling back into the cave, when Aeoma grabbed her arm. "I will shade you, Mother-sister," she said.

They came to the hole where the sun had grown bright. Aeoma tried having Bharia huddle under her, but she couldn't coax the dead woman across the sunlit floor, try as she might. Bharia's eyes rolled and she clung to the rock walls like a limpet. Nothing the girl said or did could move her. "It hurts," she moaned. "Little one, I'd forgotten how much living hurts." Suddenly she scuttled back down the path and was gone around a corner. The girl screamed her name, but the Queen was gone.

At that moment the drums suddenly started up again and the Great Door swung open, groaning on its stone hinges. There was a silence and a man walked in. Tyos was draped with heavy onyx and gold jewellery and crowned with the tall feather headdress of a King of the Great Island. He carried the great obsidian axe of office. Beneath his regalia he was pale and his gait unsteady. But his eyes narrowed, then widened in triumph as he darted forward to grab Aeoma's arm. "There you are, you little wretch!" He stank of old wine and worse.

Aeoma was numb, exhausted as he hauled her to the mouth of the cave. In the glory of sunrise, all the People were gathered below them in a long file down the twisting Path of the Dead and crowded into the Temple Valley. She saw how thin many were, how hollow and dispirited their gaze, like hers. She dimly heard Tyos bawling her name out, calling her a defiler of the holy, but it didn't interest her. And when he made her kneel, her head on the Great Altar, she awaited the axe blow, dumb as any sheep.

She was puzzled by the screams, when the hard hands gripping her let go. She lay quietly, her cheek against the cold stone, till she smelt the burning and turned.

Tyos was on his knees and the obsidian axe had shattered where it fell. Hands tight around his throat, Bharia stood above him. Her skin was blackening in the sunlight and flames already licked her hair, but she stood straight and still, eyes locked on his. "Always the impatient one, weren't you Tyos?" she cooed. "I'd have been dead inside a week. But you'd seen me recover from other sicknesses and this time your poison helped me along. And all so you could drink a little more, waste more of our people's goods on yourself and the pit you serve. But now the grave will finally return your gifts." And with that she kissed him full on the mouth. He struggled briefly, but fell limp and heavy when she released him.

"My People!" she shouted in a voice wrenched from her last store of life, "too long have you poured your goods, your labor and life's blood down this hole in a hill!" By now her dress and hair were blazing, but she faced full into the sun and continued. "The dead want none of it. The dead want only to live again. Since we cannot have that, then let us leave you!" She turned to the altar, more flame than woman, and kicked the aside the gifts arrayed there. "No more of this! Let us all rest now." Then she laid herself down like a log on the hearth and did not speak again.

Panicked by the smell of flesh burning, a nanny goat bawled. The boy holding her tether shrugged as she pulled free, then watched dully as she scampered up the hill, still bleating. A hunched woman holding a branch of thorns caught the goat's tether, then glanced back at the altar. She dropped her branch and let the nanny go again. A man at her side dropped his own thorny branch and so did another and another. As if released from a spell, the People on the hill and in the valley dropped their gifts where they stood, mouths gaping, eyes pinned to the blaze on the altar. Some moaned and wept. A few began to steal and hoard offerings, quarrelling among themselves. But many turned silently and began to walk away.

Comment

"Bharia" (for a "bh" sound, think of something between a "b" and a "v") grew out of an article I read about ancient ruins of a gigantic, elaborate

mausoleum in Malta. The authors postulated, believably in my opinion, that these ruins were vestiges of society that poured vast resources into glorifying and propitiating ancestors, up to a final social and ecological collapse. I tried to imagine what it would be like to be young in such a time and place. Parallels between such an event and the present are, of course, yours to draw, or not.

The End

DEAR METAXA

Nuke me now. So, like, here I am in Milwaukee, right? Because I didn't want to go to Ganymede with my Parental Units & play Mall Marathon with my stupid sister while Dadsy ODs on lo-grav golf (Look at the loft I get on those puppies!) & Mumsy just ODs. So the PUs decide I should visit my uncle & aunt in Wisconsin.

"It'll be fun, Drambuie. You'll learn a lot."

Excuse me, I don't really want to know how they forage for roots & berries, Mumsy-dearest. But does anyone listen?

So I'm in the airport (yeah, they call it that) & here come Unk & Ant & they're dressed to distress in His 'n' Her matching stonewashed bustier'n' tap pants outfits from Neo-Sears. It's so last nano, I mean, we're over that look now & did I mention fuck you?

& we're going out & Unk just bends down & slurps at a, pardon me, water fountain, which they've got right out in public. I was so mort!!! Then we go home to dinner. DINNER!!!

And there's, like, dihydrogenmonoxide all over the place, stuff they call "soup" & "soft drinks" & I finally realize (I am so clueless sometimes) that they expect me to INGEST this gar-bahge! As IF!!!

So I try to tell them, like, no one does, pardon me, water any more, that we're really not about that now & everybody is into hydrofluoric acid. AT LEAST. & the Ant starts, excuse me, praying & Unk is trying to talk me into TAKING OFF MY RESPIRATOR! I mean, pardon me, what planet is this?

& as if this isn't bad enough... oh, I just can't say, it's Mort City!!! OK, OK, but if Kahlua or any of those other feeblets hears about this, I swear I'll tell EVERYONE about who was doing meiosis in Language Arts Class, do I make myself clear? Well, I look around, take in the"meat" & the "soup" & the "bread" & it FINALLY HITS ME:

These people are carbon based!!!

The End

Crawling to the Moon, Page 50

COMPOST

Turning it over. Shovel biting into wetness, powdery scuzziness, raked leaves, coffee grounds and filters. Bones boiled clean for soup. Orange peels, mowed grass, potatoes gone punk.

Teresa from next door watches me.

She always seems to be out here. When the other kids are inside for the evening, windows glowing TV blue, I see her jumping the impossible hopscotch labyrinth her mother has purple chalked on the sidewalk. Or pushing her pink doll carriage down the alley in the morning before the paper comes. Playing daylong games of hide and seek, though I never see anyone looking for her but her mother.

But whatever she's doing gets dropped to come and watch me rake leaves, pick up the garbage that blows into my yard. Pull weeds. I sometimes think I should be doing something more interesting, amusing, be something different than an old man yanking a thistle, or now shouldering up spadefuls of what I mean to be earth, smutty brown stuff steaming in the morning chill.

I would like to give her something other than my carefully distanced attention when she asks her solemn questions.

"What's that?"

"Celery."

"Why do you always do this?" and that's a good one.

I'm not a gardener. It's something to do with giving back, though I can't say why it's important that it happen here, now. The same thing would go on at a landfill. There'd be more time involved, the multitude of unravellings, lives that start and lose grip and start again, so like and different from our own bodies.

But what's time to the soil?

I say I'm growing compost, food for plants. Teresa considers this. Then asks, "What do plants like to eat?"

She fiddles with her pink T-shirt, with a decal that says "Watch It!" while she waits for my answer. All her clothes seem to have a big label or message somewhere. She has three quarter-inch round scars on her belly. Old scars: they've stretched. She limps a little, too. I've tried to imagine the glowing end of the cigarette burning, the wordless scream, the fists. Maybe that's all it is, imagination.

Prefacing Middlemarch, George Eliot speaks of St. Teresa, founder of nothing, a little girl who led her small brother off on her own private crusade, toddling, hand in hand, out to liberate Jerusalem from the Saracens, a people far more civilized and humane than the Europeans who sent crazed knights and malnourished children off to die in lands they couldn't even imagine.

"Plants eat yucky things, grotty, nasty, oooogly stuff."

Teresa giggles politely."

"How come your neck swings around when you shake your head like that?"

Looking at my face, losing her smile.

Then, quiet, "What kind of yucky stuff?"

"It swings because my skin is baggy. Old people start to shrink, but their skin doesn't, so it gets crumply and loose. And you see here, this is some toast that got burnt. Here's the wrinkled-up end of a carrot. This is a prickly weed you watched me pull in the front yard. Remember, I had to go get my work gloves?"

"Uh huh" More quiet. "Sherry at daycare says weeds are just plants we don't know how to use."

"That's right, weeds are plants, too. Most of this stuff is a plant or a part of a plant."

I watch her consider this cannibalism and I want to tell her that everything is that way, eating itself and everything that's not itself. Maybe she knows already.

In The Secret House, David Bodanis talks about the ecology of our homes and yards, making the point that every conceivable area of our surroundings is home to a multitude of creatures, all constantly engaged in feeding, breeding and biochemical guerrilla warfare. I always assigned the book to first year classes. It's something I think about often, this web of hidden lives.

"But how do plants eat?"

"Well, most of the time the plant just squats there," as I sit heavily onto the brick edge of the house's empty, built-in planter, "and it waits. And it thinks. Until... one day... a little girl with some candy goes by... And it jumps up and STEALS HER LOLLIPOP!"

My talon-curled hands joined at the wrist like the jaws of the carnivorous plant in Little Shop of Horrors. Gnash gnash! Teresa squeals and dances away, then back, just close enough so the horrible jaws can snap at her again and again.

Her family moved in a couple of months ago, just before the first semester started. A little after sunset, while they were still unpacking, I invited Barry and Melanie over for a drink. Barry called Teresa, who was on the swing the last people had left. She picked up the Barbie on the seat beside her, then put it down, one little plastic hand through the chain, and set it swinging, gently. Barry put her on his shoulders, so he had to stoop way down at my door. He's one of those tall Scandinavian types, skinny, with almost invisible eyebrows and lashes. Melanie is small and dark-haired, like her daughter. She wore sunglasses and a long-sleeved blouse, though it was warm and starting to get dark. She asked me if she could smoke. I'm a pipe man, so I didn't mind. I got Teresa a lemonade. My grandchildren are all boys, older, so there wasn't much for her to play with. I showed her a Gameboy I keep for when they visit. Barry looked at my books.

"You must be the dean the real estate agent talked about." He had a smooth baritone, like a classical music radio host.

"Just a retired department head, really, and only because there wasn't anybody else around to do it."

"From your shelves, it's hard to tell whether you were in English or biology.

"Bacteriology. I minored in English and always meant to get back and do some reading. Now that I'm retired, I'm making up for lost time."

My house was built when people still socialized on the porch in the summers, so that's where we sat, in the back, to talk. Barry taught aeronautical engineering and had some commercial projects on the side, which is probably how they could afford a house in this neighbourhood.

He seemed very interested in what I thought of the university administration, which was not much or often. I tried a few times to involve Melanie and Teresa in the conversation, but Barry did most of the talking.

While we spoke he kept an eye on Teresa, once glancing over at Melanie, who silently took the Gameboy from her daughter and turned the sound off. Teresa seemed more used to computer games than I would have expected. She played Ms Pacman while we talked, quietly manipulating the little devouring jaws around the maze. After about half an hour, Barry stood up and stretched.

"Time for us to be heading home. We've got another long day ahead of us tomorrow. C'mon ladies."

Without answering, Teresa laid the Gameboy aside. In a minute, they were all out of the house, leaving nothing but three empty glasses, a full ashtray and a small screen where tiny things chased each other silently. The next day I was out on my back porch, smoking my pipe and reading when I saw Teresa in her backyard. I waved. She called me, asking if she could play again with the Gameboy. When I said yes, she came over with one of her dolls. I found her waiting for me on the back porch when I brought the little computer out. I sat down on the steps beside her.

"I noticed you played Ms Pacman yesterday. What other games do you know, Teresa?"

"I know Tetris and Donkey Kong."

While we were talking, she ducked under my arm and sat on my lap, poking at the buttons as she bounced up and down. I was transfixed, suddenly feeling how long it had been since I was last touched, this child's nonchalant weight like family. The eyes reaching for me through hedges and fences. I carefully laid my pipe aside and let her hold the game while I lifted her off my lap. I wanted to hug her. I wanted her to go away.

She said "You got bad breath, fuck."

"That's because I smoke. Also I have false teeth." I shoved the plate down with my upper lip.

She laughed delightedly.

"Sometimes food gets underneath them. Little germs start eating it and making it smell bad."

"My Mom makes me use mouthwash."

"I should probably too."

Now, at the compost heap, she stays far enough away to dodge back from gnashy hands. Progress, I think. I called Social Services yesterday. After heading down several false paths on the voice mail system, I got a social worker. She had a cold and sniffled every so often. But she listened to my suspicions, which sounded less and less substantial to me the longer I talked. She asked if I knew where the family had been living before. I said I didn't know, but would try to find out. She sounded, not bored, but as if she knew this story, the few ways it could turn out.

"How do plants really eat?" Teresa wants to know.

"Well, you see this weed? How it's not so green any more? That's because it's drying out and bacteria, little bitty plants so small we can't even see them, and eeny weeny bugs, are starting to chew it up. There's bacteria on everything in this compost heap. That's why I'm turning it over, so the bacteria can get at more of it. They chew up everything so bigger plants can put their roots down and eat it."

She looks at the compost doubtfully.

"No, Teresa, they're really, really tiny." I consider getting out a microbiology textbook to show her pictures of construction machinery-looking mites, slipper-shaped paramecia, blobby amoebae. Monsters everywhere. For centuries, European crusaders and explorers came home with stories straight out of Pliny, giant anthrophagoi, griffins and chimaera, Antipodeans with eyes in their chests. No matter where they went, their world embodied Ovid's parables, Biblical allegories, folk legends.

"What's that?"

"It's a millipede. He eats little bugs we can hardly see. He was probably down at the bottom of the compost heap and now that I've mixed it all up, he's looking for some dinner."

Teresa watches the millipede's fierce gray streaming over the heap's detritus, till it dives back under the surface. Occasionally, you can see what's coming for you. Not often, though.

"He's a funny little fucker."

"Now, is that how a little girl should talk?"

She looks at me with a calculating blankness so complete that I'm at a loss to continue.

"What's that thing?" She points to a bit of blue-green poking out of the pile.

"Gee, I don't know. Let's dig it up."

Incongruous in the compost's gray-brown, it looks like a dully aquamarine-coloured rock, though it's light on my shovel. I slice it open. And loose a boiling knot of tiny red ants, interrupted mining the inside of a moldy Kaiser bun.

"Holy" says Teresa, swallowing the "sh-" that comes after.

Someone works with her, tries to instill some small gentility in her. I wonder about her mother, Sherry at daycare. George Eliot talks about the unnoted, the ones no book mentions, who compose history's great waves with their small ripples. What about all the other ripples, I wonder, the ripples against the currents, the ripples across.

What happens to them?

"If there's little plants already in there," Teresa says slowly, "how come you keep digging it up? My mother says you should leave plants alone when they're growing."

"Your Mom's right about big plants. But the little plants I want to grow need air, and they can't get enough of that down at the bottom of the compost pile. So every so often, I turn it over."

I thought of the billions of lives, like memories, shaken loose with every spadeful, dying, maimed or somehow landing whole, snagging oxygen molecules like beach balls floating by. They've found life miles deep in the ground, thriving at crushing pressures and kiln heat. Our air is poison to them; they live on boiling sulfur, oxygen's poor cousin. Life takes what there is, even if it's brimstone.

"Look, you got a plant already." Pointing at the tender white of a shoot.

"Yeah, but that's not the kind we want, so-- "

"Don't!"

But the shovel has already chopped the seedling in half, twisted it into the wet stuff of the heap.

"Why'd you do that? It was already growing!"

"Teresa, it wasn't the right kind of plant-- "

"How do you know? Sherry says they all look the same when they're little. Maybe it was a good plant."

"That's right, Teresa, maybe it was. But right now I'm not growing plants, I'm growing compost. When the compost is done, then I'll get some seeds and grow the kind of plants I want in it. Now, how would you like some grape juice?"

She looks at me and something in her face closes, not completely, but enough.

"Sure."

The End

OUT IN THE BACKYARD

It's so still, even the honeysuckles have stopped lisping in the green steam rising out of grass.

Down in the ravine, a box turtle crawls under the big sycamore tree, the one Daddy says doesn't really have a face.

They brought the barn owl down out of its crown yesterday, all those boys with their bows. One of them pointed up, away from the round target and in a minute, he was down, his round, yellow eyes burned through in the afternoon sun.

Tiny wild strawberries raced like little wounds through the long grass and the yellowjackets buzzed around the pear tree. We didn't get out in time this year and they're buzzing there now, around the pulped, rotten pears and her.

Jeffy from across the road says the yellow jackets catch things and sting them to death, deep in their burrows. Or sometimes they just drag them down there, to lay their eggs on.

The cicadas are awake after 17 years and they're just starting to tweeze the lid off the evening, so she can move again. After holding up the pear tree's heavy shadow all day, she is bent, her feet deep in the heavy, sweet soil, where night crawlers wriggle between her toes.

In a minute, the first firefly will add his small, green note to the dark chord of the ravine and her head will come up, her eyes will open.

I'm going to go out there, tonight. I am.

The End

Crawling to the Moon, Page 58

SIDECAR

"Did you ever," the guy at the bar asked, waggling his finger in a little figure-eight, "get a chance to take back your life, the life you should have had?"

It was a slow Tuesday night at Whats-His-Face, a small bar on the fringe of Malibu. The owner was out of town and nobody fed the jukebox, so Cappy had on some quiet Thelonius Monk while he polished glasses, trying to figure how he'd do those chord substitutions differently, make it his own. Monk was great as always, but Cappy was having a hard time concentrating. He felt kind of sick, like the first tickle of a flu. Been pulling too many shifts here, he thought.

There was a knot of regulars in the corner, two agents, a line producer and someone's evil sister from a recently cancelled soap. They all seemed half asleep, chatting desultorily, momentarily free of the free-floating anxiety, petty insults and schemes that were the daily bread of a lower-end player.

The guy at the bar seemed like the only live one in the room. He had the palpable neediness of a confessing drunk, the kind who'd keep jawing on for hours about secrets Cappy really didn't want to know. Kept talking and slamming back Sidecars. He seemed familiar in a strange way. But around LA a lot of people seemed familiar, if you watched any TV at all.

The guy wasn't letting it go. "Really, Cappy my man. You don't know me, not now. Teddy Kleinschmidt, not that it matters. Like the song says, you can call me Al. Or whatever. But I took back my life. And that's a good thing, right?"

Typical narcissistic Hollywood crap. Out of the corner of his eye he saw one of the minor players making a point with that same figure-eight gesture. What a bunch of trained monkeys these Industry types were. "What do you mean, take back your life?" Cappy said, regretting the words as he said them, but committed now. "It's your life. Nobody can take it from you. They can kill you, but the only one can give your life away is you."

"That's what they always say. Work hard, do your best, keep your nose clean and you'll get ahead. Master of your own destiny. Rooty-toot-toot. But I'm here to tell you that someone took my life away. And I got it back. Along with everyone else's."

"Your own life and everybody else's life too? Whatever, man." Not even bothering to feign interest, Cappy started loading the dishwasher.

"These days it's all 'been there, done that'. Might as well be talkin' to yourself. That's why I like comin' here. Good old Whats-His-Face and Cappy, a refuge from all that doppelganger crap. I've caught you playing at Bonesy's, you know. You're a hell of a pianist, really got something of your own there."

Embarrassed by praise where he'd expected only irritation, Cappy managed "Gee, thanks a lot." Was he blushing or just feverish?

"Hey, you know it's true. Nobody can take that from you, right? With you I know I'm talking to another person, another soul in life's...." he waved vaguely. "You think I'm going to start blathering about Method acting, how I Become My Character and so reach universal... whatever. Or maybe I'm going to hand you some We-Are-The-World mystical hoo-ha. But I really only wanted to be one guy. And I did it. Everybody else was just.... Set me up with another Sidecar, if you'd be so kind."

"Comin' up." If you'd be so kind, Cappy thought, reaching for the Triple Sec. How many times had he heard that in the last few days? Some new exec starts making waves at Disney or wherever and in a few days they're all using his little pet phrases. That and Sidecars. Every third-string soap actor and minor network flunkie was suddenly drinking Sidecars. One step up from a girl drink, in Cappy's opinion, which nobody asked.

One of the agents sneezed. Everybody seemed to have a cold these days. Cappy felt a tickle in his throat again. He took a sip of tonic water.

"You're probably saying to yourself 'why do I get all the wackos in here?'"

"Nah, Los Angeles's got more nutjobs per capita than anywhere else. This city'd grind to a halt without its crazies. They gotta get a drink somewhere."

"Truer words were never spoken. But I'm telling you the God's Own Truth. I wanted to be Damon Sheehan and I did it."

Now he had it figured out. A few nights ago he'd come home from jamming in an after-hours joint. He remembered how excited he'd been. He'd been hot. Better, though, was that he'd surprised himself. Made the piano do things that didn't sound like anyone but him. He'd have gone on longer, but all the players had day jobs, including him. Charged up, unable to sleep, he'd turned on the tube, trying to zone out. What he'd got was an interview with Damon Sheehan on some star-worshipping show. The actor had been talking about his newest role in some thriller. Every so often he'd waggle his finger in a little figure-eight to make a point.

"So you're Damon Sheehan." He looked the guy over. Probably went about 5'8". Thin ginger hair over a pale, somewhat popeyed, slope-jawed face. Puffy cheeks scarred from acne. Well-cut casual silk suit that couldn't disguise poor posture and a small but definite potbelly.

"You're thinking, Damon Sheehan, huh? Where's the great hair, the jaw, those piercing eyes, the pecs, the biceps, the--"

"I can walk away if you want a moment to yourself here."

"Hey, I'm no stalker, no matter what his lawyers'll tell you. I grew up with the jerk when he was still Danny Shynkiw."

"Right, you're not a stalker. You Knew Him When."

"We lived six doors apart in Winnipeg. He was the bully of my neighborhood. He used to take my lunch money from me whenever he caught me on the way to school. It's a good thing he played hooky so much or I'd never have had anything to eat."

"Aw. Bad scene."

"This isn't a poor-me story, Cappy. I told you I got him and I did."

"He looked OK when I saw him on TV the other night."

"Thanks, and I mean that. The worst thing wasn't that nobody believed me, although they didn't, not much. It was that even when he was caught dead to rights, he could laugh or charm his way out of it. High school was like a foreign country where he was a king and I was in exile. He'd repeat the same joke I'd just told and get a bigger laugh. He'd elbow me in gym class and the coach would turn a blind eye. He'd get caught because he'd forced me to do his homework and the teacher would blame me. Nobody could believe that handsome, athletic Danny was a sadistic sociopath. And if he beat up a little loser or two, well, boys will be boys."

"For something that's not a sob story, I'm hearin' a lot of violins."

"Just wait. What really got him was how easy school was for me. Math and science, chemistry especially. Danny wasn't stupid, but he had a hustler's intelligence. He read people quickly, figured out their weaknesses and acted ruthlessly. Systems, abstractions, anything counter-intuitive defeated him. The chem lab was the physical manifestation of everything he couldn't understand. It was the one place I could escape him. It scared him. I made sure of that when he tried to grab me there and I threw some nitric acid at him. Hit him on his arm and started burning through his leather jacket. He howled like a kicked dog and ran to the washroom. Still has a scar.

"He left me alone after that and I managed to get through twelfth grade without too much flak from his crowd. I didn't go to football games, where we won the City championships with him as our quarterback, or basketball, where he was our star shooting guard, or track, where he set a hurdles record. He didn't pay any attention to math, chemistry or biology, where I was winning awards.

"Then came graduation. They made me valedictorian. Nobody really wanted to. I was a terrible public speaker and they didn't care what I had to say anyway. I just had the grades and awards. Danny scraped through with a C+ average. Surprisingly, he came to my speech and didn't cut up with his jock buddies. He sat looking sober and impressed, then jumped up and clapped when I was finished.

"By this time I had a girlfriend, Cindy Godey. She was a bit taller than me in heels, and pretty if you like slim brunettes with an overbite. She wrote bookish, melodramatic poetry and got straight A's in English and French. She told me she hated sports. We hadn't done anything beyond some frustrating, awkward petting but I was hoping.

"Grad night was the way I suppose they all are, hokey and enormously exciting. In a badly-fitted rental tux I danced woodenly with Cindy, made stilted small talk with one of the teachers, got mildly drunk on some vodka one of my Math Club buddies had smuggled in and exulted silently: I was finally getting out of this place, away from the tyranny of my school's Jockocratic caste system and into the world. I was going to win a McArthur Fellowship, a Nobel. Cindy would be a Pulitzer-winning poet and my loving wife. I was going to get laid tonight.

"Cindy seemed preoccupied, but I put it down to the night's excitement and the new life ahead of her. I saw her giving me speculative glances now and then. I say I saw her now, but really at the time I barely noticed, I was so keyed up.

"Danny came with the Prom Queen, Marcie Smythe, a stacked blonde rich girl, on his arm. They danced a couple of numbers, then left in a stretch limo for some Beautiful People's party or other. I hardly noticed them, except in the way you admire magazine models, pretty but not anything to do with you.

"Finally it was time to leave. I had it all planned. We were going to swing by Itzy Berlinger's apartment, I'd told Cindy, because I had to feed his cats. Itzy was a violinist whose daughter I'd tutored in math and chem. They were away now because he was playing in Tel Aviv. What I hadn't told Cindy was that I'd stocked the place with nice nibblies, chilled some of Itzy's champagne and lined up the most romantic-sounding albums of his impressive collection. I wasn't leaving anything to chance.

"It went just the way I wanted, up to a point. That point was where Cindy turned to me and said 'Teddy, I have something to tell you.' A few days ago she'd 'just happened' to run into Danny at the library. He was very polite but seemed troubled. They went for coffee and Danny 'poured out his soul' to her. He told her how lucky she was to have such a brilliant guy and how he wished he could be like me. He was 'deeply sorry' for everything he put me through, which he now realized had been only from envy. Of all the people in school, he said, I was the one he most wished for as a friend. And now, because of his own stupidity and immaturity, that would never happen. He hoped that she, Cindy, would forgive him. She'd see him at the Grad dance with Marcie Smythe, but his heart would be with us, wishing us well.

"He played her like Itzy played a violin. The upshot was that Cindy said she 'needed some time to think'. I drove her home like a zombie.

"Next day he got her drunk at a party at his folk's place on the lake and screwed her silly. I know because he sent me the videotape he made with a hidden camera."

"Sweet."

"Don't worry. He got his."

"So you keep saying. What happened to Cindy?" "

"Oh, he threw her over after a couple of weeks, when his football scholarship to Kansas came through. She called me. She's got a couple of kids now. Divorced. Still calls me, once in a while. We've talked, but somehow..." He waved his hand vaguely again, a gesture that seemed oddly familiar.

"OK, wait a minute." Cappy took a long drink of tonic water. "Does it seem hot in here tonight?"

"Lot of people running a low-grade fever these days. You were saying?"

"Well, it's high school. Nasty people get away with nasty things in high school. But you get through it. I mean you're wearing a nice suit now and you don't have to deal with the jerk any more. You don't really, do you?"

"No, I'm not in any deals that involve Damon Sheehan, if that's what you're asking. Not now."

"There you go. Ancient history."

"That's what I told myself. I got over Cindy about the time I got a scholarship to Caltech. I figured biotech was where the most fruitful research was and I did great. Two years at Caltech, one in London, another in Tokyo, then back to Caltech. I was hot property. I'd discovered that the brain makes memories in the same way some viruses act on cells. Not only that, but I was on my way to figuring how to duplicate the process. My prof was trying to claim my basic research as his own, so I quit and started my own company.

"Memenda's stock went through the roof ten minutes after initial offering. These were the days of the dotcom millionaires and those guys thought we were uber-cool. What we were offering was the promise of memories. Imagine learning Shakespeare with a pill or calculus through an injection. It was a way down the road, everybody knew, but before the bubble burst people wanted to be in on the dream.

"Danny got hurt at Kansas and lost his starting position. The day I made my first personal mil, one of the secretaries got me lit on rock cocaine, among other things. I thought I was God, a Vengeful God. I looked him up and fedexed him a few clippings about me and Memenda, just to rub his nose in it.

"No forgiving or forgetting with you, is there?"

"I'm not proud of it, but it seemed like a tiny bit of payback at the time. It wasn't, as things turned out."

"How did they turn out?"

"Badly. What I didn't know was that along with acting, Danny was preparing for a career change by romancing Bebe Costanza's daughter."

"Costanza, isn't he the guy..."

"Who produced "Sword of Damocles", "The Pentagram", "The Calling" and a few other hits that didn't happen to star Damon Sheehan. Yeah, that's him. Also CEO of Apexor, one of Memenda's biggest investors."

"Uh oh."

"Yeah, the day they tied the knot Danny called me personally to let me know that Apexor was selling our stock off. It couldn't have come at a worse time. I had just started building a house, a big house and was extended to the max. Memenda had acquired a number of very specialized, expensive pieces of hardware that we were struggling to calibrate and bring up to production.

"The air was coming out of the dotcom bubble and everybody was nervous. The news that Apexor was selling sealed our doom. There was run on our stock and after two days I was left with some extremely hard-to-sell machines depreciating as I watched and a half-poured foundation on some land I had no hope of paying for.

"In the midst of this I had an insight. I always seem to have them when the pressure's at the max. I don't know why. I saw that I could use a tailored virus to trace out the brain's essential memories, transforming itself into a kind of memory imprint. Using a number of viruses, I could record a personality, its drives and memories. I just needed time and money to develop it."

"What an idea to get when your back was to the wall."

"You know it, Cappy. The first thing I did was swallow my pride and go to Apexor. I begged them for an extension, said I would work as an employee, that I'd forego any patent rights.

"They scheduled a meet with me at Wing Ping's, a Szechuan joint where all the top Silicon Valley guys eat when they aren't pulling all-nighters. At first I thought it was a good sign.

"Then I arrived and found Danny was chairing the meeting, if that's what you call a public execution. He laughed in my face, said my research was a dead end, that Apexor wouldn't be interested if I promised them Eternal Life. He did it at Wing Ping's to let everyone know I was finished."

"OK, OK, I'm listening, but I gotta go to the head and Louise, my regular girl, called in sick. Could you watch the bar for me?"

"Sure thing, Cappy."

While the bartender was gone Teddy lounged back, surveying the room. The actress coughed, then caught his eye and waggled her finger in a figure-eight at him. He smiled and nodded.

In ten minutes Cappy was back, sweating profusely. "Sorry man," he said. "I lost my supper in there. Must be coming down with stomach flu or something. I might have to close up early if it doesn't get better. I really don't feel like myself."

"Yeah, something's going round. Listen, why don't you have a seat and I'll fix you something to pick you up before closing. Here, you go." He helped Cappy onto one of the stools. "Man, you're shaking like a leaf. What'll you have?"

"All of a sudden, I feel like a Sidecar."

"You know, somehow I knew you were going to say that. Coming up."

"Seems like everybody's drinking them these days. I never used to like them myself. I never liked brandy or Triple Sec. But just now I'm craving one. What's with that?"

"People's tastes change, I guess. How's that?"

"Oh, that's good. I feel a bit better too."

"Funny, isn't it? Must be the whiskey sour mix or something. So anyway, after that meeting, I was basically at the bottom."

"OK, is this going to take long? I said I was better, but that's a long way from good."

"This'll be over by the time you finish your drink. Besides, you're going want to hear the end."

"OK man. Go."

"So when I finally picked myself up, I went back to academia. Called in all the favors I was ever owed and then some. I was doing whatever I can, guest-lecturing here, lab assisting there, begging and scraping for lab time anywhere. They gave me stuff mostly out of pity. After the crash, everyone figured I'd lost it.

"The funny thing was they were right, just not the way everyone thought. I was sick. Pancreatic cancer, not aggressive, not then. But if you read up on all your miracle cures, and I have, you'll find a conspicuous absence of anything that stops that one. It's a sure-fire killer.

"And all the while I was doing my research on the quiet. Oh, I had a cover story for my lab time. Something safe, but a bit dotty. But what I was really doing is cooking up what I called my Viromemes. Hundreds of them, all based on an air-borne infector, each responsible for mapping out a different area of the brain. All of them tailored for Danny, for his blood type and some other factors that made him virtually the only target. They were engineered to wipe me out as they recorded, then rewrite me over his brain when they got there."

"I gotta say, this sounds pretty nuts."

"I wasn't particularly sane at the time. But it worked, more or less."

"More or less?"

"I went home and dosed myself up. I made sure I was lousy with them. I could feel them stripping my brain clean. Can you imagine what it's like to have things vanish from your memory as you're thinking of them?"

"So far all I've heard is an elaborately weird plan for mental suicide. And you're still here."

"After two days, I had a timed bot in my computer send out a press release to all major media outlets, making a lot of scurrilous claims about Damon Sheehan and Apexor, some of them even true. Danny didn't even bother showing up. He sent a really nasty piece of work, a lawyer named of Al Kouralt, to serve me with a summons.

"He got into my house easily. But I had the door rigged so he had to spend 20 minutes with a comatose, infected body before he could get out and take a meeting with Danny.

"And now I'm him. I infected the creep and I'm Damon Sheehan. I've got his mansion, his Lamborghini collection, his gorgeous wife and his even hotter girlfriend. Or alternatively, the guy you see on the screen, he's just a pretty simulacrum, a nice package for Teddy Kleinschmidt."

"Um, my friend, have you looked in the mirror lately?"

"It's a funny thing about that. I was so intent on perfecting the viral mapping function and making sure they were really virulent that I may have slipped up on making them Danny-specific. Or maybe they mutated. All I know is I woke up a couple of weeks ago in this body. Say hello to Al Kouralt. I assume he's still in there somewhere. I've got a bunch of his memories, along with mine. It gets a bit confusing at times.

"Of course in the meantime, he and Danny had been making contacts right and left. You can't beat a couple of big-time Industry players for really efficient disease vectors. And once infected, those other vectors have been going into the world, spreading the word, as it were. It's causing some changes, though nobody else seems to have caught on to it yet, and we're not telling. In Mali, for example, the President and the chief rebel leader have suddenly declared a truce worked out through a mutual love of Sidecars. Which is kind of awkward, both being Muslims and all... Prison guards and death row prisoners are sitting down and talking about genetic theory as we speak. The Pope just handed down an encyclical in favor of stem cell research.

"Now you're thinking we're taking over the world, right? But really everything is the same, just different. All the bodies, they do what their situations warrant. Hookers are hookers, judges, midwives, farmers, we all do what we've been doing. I never was much of wave-maker, really. Everybody's got their own old memories, just some more on top, is all. We're not telepathic or anything weird. Hell, sometimes we don't even like each other. Plus it looks like some people are developing antibodies, or maybe just don't react to me. Which is a relief, to tell you the truth. I'm not much of a cook, and some of the restaurant meals I've been getting lately... well, I just hope there are a few chefs out there with an immunity. And I wish I were a better piano player..."

"OK, this is just too wacked. And it's closing time, finally. Not a moment too soon. I feel like hammered shit."

"My advice to you, Cappy, is go home and get a good sleep. Tomorrow you'll feel like a new man."

Comment

Here's a story about revenge served really cold, and the consequences.

We've all had the experience, at one time or another, of being the one person in the room who isn't clued into what's happening, who doesn't get it. "Sidecar" suggests that maybe you might not want it, all things considered. Or maybe you do, since everyone else has already got it. It's hard to say. Maybe just have another drink, and don't think too hard about it.

The End

THE BIG ROCK CANDY MOUNTAIN

We were halfway to the train in a black Manitoba squall when the railroad bull saw us. He gave a yell, didn't even hardly sound human, and come running, boots sloshing through the mud. Through whipping curtains of rain I couldn't see him clear, but he held something I took to be a shotgun. Why he wasn't in the station house waiting out the storm, I don't know. I guess Fascism never sleeps, like Trotsky says.

It was raining cold and mean, howitzer thunder shivering the night. Orry was having a conniption, wheezing and spitting blood. I was back Over There, artillery surf pounding me into the trenches, into the mud with the rats. I could feel that cop's eyes on my back, an itch I couldn't scratch, like I always could when a sniper lined me up at Vimy. But we ran in the dark railyard, dodging through those tunnels in France, Orry rasping hup, hup, and me half dragging, half carrying him. And I ran and reached and reached and finally just managed to shoulder him into the black doorway of an empty boxcar.

Orry flopped down like a sack of spuds, too done even to reach for me. And I thought right, this is where I lose him. I was through myself, sick with the runs from bad Mulligan stew in a hobo jungle outside The Soo, back in Ontario. The big iron knuckles between the cars clanked and pounded like mortar fire and my gasping breaths hurt down to my crotch. I'll just stop here, I thought. Lie down in the cold, wet weeds, let that bull catch me and wake up in the Big Rock Candy Mountains.

And I would've, too. Far ahead, the engine had hit straight track and was picking up speed around the bend. I was losing pace with Orry. I could see his pale face in the moonlight, moving off. He was trying to say something to me, but I couldn't hear it. I could hear the bull's boots behind me, thudding closer. I tripped over something--

--and felt myself caught, just when the rocky ground leaped up at me. For a moment, whoever had me just let me dangle, weeds, mud and granite track ballast blurring past my eyes. Then I felt a ripple and got pulled in, turning over and over. I caught sight of the bull for a second--what with his slicker blowing and crackling in the hard rain he looked more like some jellyfish than a man--and he tripped over something too, I guess, because he went down like he'd hit a wall. Then he was up, howling like a fiend. Fired a shot in desperation. Something clipped me hard in the shoulder. Why a man with a good job would get so upset at a couple 'boes jumping a train on a night like that... Capitalism makes a body mean, like Joe Hill says.

Then I was in the dark of the boxcar, being laid down gentle on a pile of straw. Dry too, for a wonder, the first dry thing I'd felt in seemed like days. Smelled so fine, like fresh hardtack biscuit. That and something else, hard to put a name to. Somewhere between fish and lilacs, if that makes any sense. I felt my shoulder underneath my shirt. It was maybe a little bruised, but nothing had broken the skin. There was a hard little lump in the shoulder padding of my greatcoat. But I didn't think much of that, except to count my blessings for Army tailors.

I could hear breathing beside me, loud and hoarse, the way he done since he took mustard gas at Ypres. "You OK, Orry?" I asked, when I got my wind back.

"Never better," he rasped back. "Let our friend here know that we appreciate his assistance." Orry could only talk just above a whisper, so he relied on me for speechifying.

"Stranger," I said, raising my voice against the thudding and squeaking of the train "we're much obliged for your hospitality. I'm Liam Carmichael of the Come by Chance Carmichaels and my pal here is Orry, or Orest Shevchenko, to speak more proper, from Saskatoon."

Silence, or as much silence as you can have in a moving boxcar in a thunderstorm. I suddenly wondered how it was so warm and toasty in here, without no fire.

"In other words", I said, trying to fill up space, "a salt-cod Newfie b'y from the Blue Puttees and a sawed-off Ukrainian sodbuster who served with the Princess Pats. And to whom do we owe this ride and comfort?"

Another silence. Then a sigh, or something like. I felt the boxcar shift, just a tiny bit, as if something mighty heavy had moved to one side of it. Then there was a low light, from where I couldn't tell you exactly. It played over a face, sort of, and a body taking up near half the car.

He looked like a man, if you weren't too particular. Two eyes, anyway, and a mouth down below. Nothing much like a nose or hair. Two arms and legs, but not jointed any way I seen before. He was decked out in gear with all kinds of pockets and gewgaws, all looking the worse for wear. He lay sprawled out on a bedroll, back propped up on a big duffle bag.

There was loads of equipment surrounding him, mostly things I could hardly describe, let alone put a use to. But near to hand he had something glittery and kind of small, for the size of him. It didn't resemble anything I'd ever laid eyes on before, but I know a gun when I see it.

And I couldn't say what his kind was supposed to look like new, but seemed to me he'd been banged around and scuffed up considerable. He drew in another breath and spoke in a voice like wind through a cornfield, "I'm not from anywhere around here. I go by Billy, on this planet."

I swallowed, then stuck out my paw. I maybe hadn't seen much stranger, but there was lots worse in the trenches. Besides, I might be shell-shocked and wake up sure the Boches have lobbed a mortar round into my bedroll, but I don't take fright easy when I'm awake.

And Orry, he was so close to final roll call that nothing much fazed him. He shook hands with Billy like putting his mitt in a big greenish mangle-looking thing that folded up three ways was something he did every day. Then he reached into his greatcoat and brought out that mickey of gin we got from a bootlegger in Ignace. There was only a swallow or two left, but he offered it to the stranger. Orry is a stickler for what's proper.

Crawling to the Moon, Page 73

Billy ducked that big knobby head of his, took the bottle and finished her off. When he shifted to do that his suit did something that gave me the heebies. A little tube came snaking out of one part of it on the left, then dived down lower on the right. I looked close and I could tell that underneath there was a big chunk of him missing. There was a hole in his jacket and I could see underneath to some gray lumpy stuff. I'm no sawbones, but those were field dressings, sure as you're born. He swallowed that gin, and all of a sudden the cold wind rushed through that boxcar, fit to yank the life right of you.

Then Billy reached into a big crate by his side and pulled out a bottle full of something cloudy that glowed a bit in the dark, sort of purply. He cracked it open and took a shot. Just as suddenly as it turned cold, that boxcar was warm as a Christmas parlor. He passed the bottle over.

Orry, he didn't look any too happy about it, but he brung that bottle up to his kisser. And damned if he didn't take a big, healthy swallow, more than I seen him keep down in quite a while.

I found out why when he handed it to me. You heard folk calling something meat and drink to them? Well, this bung-yer-eye was that and salad, hash browns, mince pie and a cigar on the veranda, afterwards. Made you feel all fortified and peaceful at the same time. A puddock full of that yogoba, I think Billy called it, and you'd never want for aught.

That improved the general tone of conversation considerable. Now having met up with a fellow not from this world, you'd think Orry and me'd be just afire with this question and that. And we did ask him a few posers. Me more than Orry, who straightaway saw eye-to-eye with the stranger. Which was right odd, being as Orry had told me he'd never been anywhere bigger than Regina before he found himself shipped to France, where the only thing he liked was the cognac.

But Billy had that effect on you. He was nine feet tall, olive green, arms that coiled like a snake and more human than a good many plain men I've met. Especially those bastard Brit officers who threw Canadian and Newfoundland boys into places they'd never even dream of sticking their own precious Limey troops.

I found myself telling him about coming home to Come by Chance and finding my sweetheart and folks dead of the Influenza.

And telling him about the Revolution and how it would bring us the Workers' Paradise. Orry laughed, like always, only heartier than he had since he come down with the consumption. Said I was just a half-cocked instigator, palavering about the Big Rock Candy Mountain. Billy just looked sad.

Instead of getting my back up, like usual, I laughed right back. Then I hauled out the concertina from my pack, pumped her up and sang:

In the Big Rock Candy Mountains there's a land that's fair and bright
Where the handouts grow on bushes and you sleep out every night
Where the boxcars are all empty and the sun shines every day
On the birds and the bees and the cigarette trees
Where the lemonade springs where the bluebird sings
In the Big Rock Candy Mountains

Midway through, Billy joined in. He had a big, deep voice, like the pedal tones on an organ. And didn't we have a proper shivaree after that, me singing and playing the squeezebox, with Orry on the spoons. He even jigged a little, which'll tell you how much that yogoba had improved his constitution, if only for a brief spell. Once Billy took a turn in the lead. He pulled out a contraption that was hard to focus on directly and played us some off-world tzigane sort of music, mighty wild and mournful. You didn't have to know the words to understand it was about love and dire fate and beauty lost forever.

We were silent for a while then, until I had to ask the question that had been devilling me since I got into that boxcar. "Uh, beg pardon, Billy, but whereabouts do you hail from, specifically?"

He looked at me with those strange tear-shaped eyes for a bit. "Liam", he said, "I'm from the War."

And like a triflin' chucklehead, I tried to make a joke of it. "Well, you best hie to homeward right quick, b'y," I said, "because they signed the Armistice last year in 1918."

Another silence. Then Billy sighed again. "Here, Liam. On this world they signed a treaty, for a while."

"How's that again?"

"Have you heard of the French and Indian Wars, Liam?"

"Have I? Where the French and Micmacs took St. John's and we took Acadia? B'y, if there was nothing else you learned in history class, they crammed that one into your skull."

"Then you might know they were just one part of what historians call the War of Spanish Succession. In other words, a quarrel between a few bluebloods in Europe that killed tens of thousands of people in places those kings and nobles never heard of, nor cared about if they did." If anyone ever asks me what a moon man sounds like when he's bitter, I'll be able to say. "Now think about your war, The War to End All Wars, as they're calling it. Millions dead, and more in the cholera and influenza that followed. And all through the years leading up to it, what were all your politicians saying? 'Nobody wants to go to war. Nobody.' But it happened anyway. Who wanted it?"

"Now hold up," said Orry. "You're saying Liam and I were shot, gassed, laid out with trenchfoot and whooping cough because of troublemakers from other planets? What do we have that you people want, if you've got ships to fly around the stars and that? And if you do want something we have, why don't a bunch of you come to take it?"

"There are more of us here than anyone knows, Orry." He fiddled with some buttons on his suit. Suddenly he was a Yank doughboy, smoking a cigarette and sporting one of those big American grins. Then he reached down and he was Prime Minister MacKenzie King at a desk, signing a piece of paper. Then himself again. It was cold when he'd finished, and damp. He took a pull of Yogoba and it warmed up, but not as fast as the first time.

"Most of us want what you want: To go home, even if home isn't there any more."

At this point, I needed to relieve myself. I nodded to the both of them and made my way over to the sliding door, which Billy had closed to keep out the rain. I eased it open and did my business. Smoked my first cigarette of the new day.

It was a clear, cold morning, dawn coming the way it does in Saskatchewan, so gentle and slow over the wheat fields, you almost forget there's a terrible white sun behind it. A red harvester was coming down the road by the track, pulled by a team of three Shires and a mule. The stoker was already hard at work, but the driver and field hands gave me a wave.

You'd think I'd be all in a sweat about what Billy told us, wondering if it was true and who could I tell and whatnot. Truth was it was just too big to think about right then. Besides, I was full of yogoba and feeling no pain.

I figured Orry and I'd be in Moose Jaw by tonight. I was going to get a job in the stockyards or some such and the dry air would help ease the consumption in Orry's lungs. Maybe he could even pick up a job dealing in one of the casinos the gangsters ran around there. For a Bohunk who'd never played anything wilder than pinochile before he enlisted, Orry took to poker like a man born for five card stud.

Then out of nowhere I felt that itch I got when a sniper took my range. I ducked to one side, sweating cold. Leaned up behind the door, waiting for my heart to slow. It came to me gradually this was different. Oh, he was out there all right, and looking for me. But he was farther off than I thought at first and couldn't sight me directly. Yet. I had a sudden vision of a beat-up Model T running a long way off, but making up time whenever the freight stopped or was sidetracked. I tried to see the driver but couldn't through the glare off the windshield.

When I stepped back Orry was nodding off and Billy was singing something low and easing, but he stopped when he saw my face. "He's getting closer, isn't he?" was what he finally said. I nodded, not sure of what I'd seen and how he knew.

He reached into one of his pockets and pulled out what looked like a little piece of metal that unfolded into a kind of shiny blanket. He spread that over Orry, then wet his finger with some of that yogoba. He put a dot of it in the middle of Orry's forehead. I could hear my pal's breathing gradually change from a gasp and hiss to a deep, regular snore.

Then Billy motioned me closer and picked up that deadly glittering little gun. He pressed something and it started making a low hum. He waved it all around me, then stopped when it began to squeal as it got close to my shoulder.

Shaking his head gently, he said to me "I'd be obliged if you would take off your coat for a moment, Liam.

I handed it over and he felt around the padding for a bit, then pinched it between fingers as thick as my wrist. The squealing stopped.

As Billy handed my coat back, he explained as how I'd been shot with a special bullet. It put out energy kind of like Madame Curie talked about, so someone with the right equipment could follow it. He said the being who shot me would be along directly. The enemy, he called it.

"But that was just a railroad bull with a shotgun."

"And I'm MacKenzie King, if I want to be. You had a closer look than that, Liam. Your people and mine are always trying to shove things in boxes they don't fit. You didn't see him too clearly, back there, but you saw enough. That wasn't a man, by most of your definitions."

I thought about that for a while. "Sorry to bring trouble on you, Billy. What do you plan to do? Can we help?"

"Well, this train is going past Crow's Nest Pass, close to where we hid a starship in a cave. You never know but I might make it there and home." He smiled, but it was the look of a gambler trying to buy the pot on a pair of threes. "Otherwise, what I aim to do is share a jug or two with my pals and swap a few lies."

"But--"

"Liam, I'm done fighting and I won't run." He straightened up and I could tell he wasn't as strong as when I'd seen him first. There were little blue lights winking on and off in his uniform. Whatever they meant, I had a hunch it wasn't good. He smiled when he saw the look on my face. "Buck up, soldier. I've had a better run than many and stories to tell. My closest buddy from the old troop is 3000 light-years away and my mate, my wife, has left me for another. So what say we have another drink and trade some yarns?"

So that's what we did. He told me about being trained to come here and how they injected languages and history into his brain like we put a letter in a post box. I told him about fishing off a dory and how ma and da saved up to send me to Jesuit school in St John's. He described his first time off his planet, how scared he'd been and how his sergeant bully-ragged him. I related as how I'd joined up, marched and trained with a wooden rifle, mostly, and shipped out, green as grass, to the trenches. He told me about his years fighting the enemy here.

It was funny, but he didn't seem to bear them any grudges. I hate them. I know that Jerry is just a man like me, tricked into fighting his working brothers by the Rockefellers and such, but I hate them and I can't help it.

Billy took the longer view. He talked about battles and you could tell he was proud, not just of his own kind, but of the enemy, how fierce and tough they were, how honorable.

By this time Orry was waking up. He staggered to the door and did the necessary, coughing so it hurt to listen. Then he spat out a big loogie, wiped his mouth, and reeled back. He took a pull of yogoba. Then sat down with a thump, the devil in his eye, like I imagine he had when he charged a machinegun nest and took out ten men by himself. And nothing would do but he had to tell the one about going on leave in Lyon and capturing a German Oberstleutnant in a whorehouse. Except that he started it this time way back when he enlisted in Regina. He did the voices of the recruiting sergeant, his mates in the Princess Pats, his snotty English lieutenant. It came to me that he was telling this one for the last time and he wanted to do it up right.

Then Billy told about fighting a long battle on three worlds and in between, the strange cities he'd been in, the wild and terrible people he'd met. They talked and they drank and they talked some more, a fierce little Ukie from the bald prairie and a giant warrior from a great space empire, two creatures whose only need now was to be heard this once, and maybe understood, a little.

This went on for I really can't say how long. I lost track of time. A few times I joined in with stories of my own, but mostly I listened. And the more Yogoba you drank, the realer the stories got to be. I think sometimes Orrie was talking in Ukrainian and Billy in his own lingo. It didn't matter. I could see Orry's Baba and smell the cooking turnips in the sod hut where he was born. I could feel it in my stomach and skin when Billy talked about floating in space, no up or down, no sound but what your body made, no soft curtain of atmosphere between you and the crystalline blaze of the stars.

The stories stretched for hours, maybe days. They compared experiences, nodded, sometimes even cried together. Or they laughed. Billy's laugh was like an earthquake, fit to shake the boxcar to pieces. I might be there still, but at some point I had to hit the latrine. They were so deep in talk that they barely noticed me going.

I eased the door open. After so long in the dimness of the boxcar, it was a shock to stand in brilliant Alberta sunlight. Moose Jaw was long gone. We were well into the foothills, I judged. Above the pines I saw a snow-capped peak off to the west. I thought about the Big Rock Candy Mountain. The song has cigarette trees and cops with wooden legs. But the first thing, the one everyone remembers, is a mountain made out of the simplest, sweetest thing in the world, the candy you got when your ma took you to the fair and a man in a brightly painted booth chucked your chin and called you sonny.

I was thinking about this and other things when he hit me. He must've been on the roof. He swung in like an ape over a branch and knocked me arse over teakettle into the plank wall of the boxcar. Then he flipped over and landed on the floor. He didn't look like anything meant to live on land. He was all blue-green flippers and tentacles, with internal organs pulsing under translucent skin. He was holding something I could see looked nothing like a shotgun. But I didn't want it pointed at me.

He said something loud, or at least made noise somewhere between a roar, a train whistle and boiling water. There might have been words in there somewhere. I don't know. I was too busy reaching for the knife I keep in my boot.

I was just pulling it out when Billy rasped "Stand easy, Carmichael. You too, Shevchenko." I looked and saw that Orry had his service revolver to hand, but Billy was blocking his aim with a massive hand. "My enemy has something he wants to say."

He did, too. He put that ray-gun, or whatever it was, over his head, talking all the while in that crashing mumbo-jumbo. Then he sort of swung it in four different directions, up and down. It didn't do my nerves no good, but at least he wasn't aiming it.

In the sunlight I could tell he'd seen some hard times. He had one long, chewed-on looking antenna and just the stump of another. His body was dulled and pitted like a spud going bad. One of his flippers was torn. He listed a bit to the left, like a man with a gimp leg. His breathing bubbled and wheezed. But he waved that weapon around like he'd used it many times and meant business.

Then he laid it down, ceremonial like, on the floor of the boxcar between him and Billy. And he did something you'd have to call a bow. In turn, Billy nodded and raised a bottle of yogoba.

I said not much fazed Orry, but his jaw was hanging halfway to the floor. Mine too, I guess. I wasn't any more collected when that creature turned to me and gave another roaring, wheezing speech.

"He asks me to let you know that he apologizes for hitting you. He was afraid you were standing guard and would raise the alarm before he could say what he needed to say," Billy translated. "He also begs you to accept his apologies for not saying this in your own language, but he is too weary and sick to do so."

Dumbly, I nodded.

Then Billie said something to the creature in that space lingo and raised the bottle again. He motioned to Orrie to make some room. The creature settled in like he was on an old friend's back porch. He hunkered down on the boxcar's pinewood floor, wrapped his tentacle around the bottle and took a mighty swig. Then he passed it to Billy, who did the same.

I was about to join them when Billy held up a big greenish hand. "We're coming into Canmore, unless I miss my guess. This is where you get off, Liam. You're young and you've got years ahead of you, years none of the rest of us have. This isn't a trip for the living." He reached into that crate and pulled out an unopened bottle of yogoba. "Keep this for when you need it," he said.

I opened my mouth to protest, looked at Orry and saw he wasn't my pal no more. Oh, he was still the fierce little guy who'd stuck up for me when no one else would, who'd watched my back in hobo jungles and on the road. But now he was a man going where I couldn't go, saying goodbye to friends and places he'd never see again. Without a word he handed me his service revolver and his Victoria Cross. Then he grabbed my hand and pumped it hard, a handshake meant to last. I had tears in my eyes and I thought he was pretending not to notice. But he reached up and dabbed them dry with a hankie. Then he gave me a shove, sat down in a corner and wouldn't look up.

I heard the engine whistle and could feel the wheels slowing as we came into the station.

Billy took my arm and said "I'd give you something else, but everything I've got would either be no use to you or get you in trouble. But I think our new friend has something that could come in handy." And there, fanned out on a box beside me, was a thousand dollars in twenties.

The creature passed the bottle over. I didn't much like doing it, but I took a pull without wiping it off. And I felt all right again, for a time. He made one of his booming speeches and Billy said. "He says he wants you to take this money, find yourself a home and a woman. And when you hold your children in your arms, please remember him."

So I jumped off that train at the yard in Canmore. There was a railroad bull on duty, but he saw that service revolver stuck in my belt and he backed off. He was just a man.

I asked him where I could find a good hotel in town. I knew he wanted to sneer at me but I looked him in the eye and he thought better of it. He told me how to get there and I started down the road.

As I was going the train started to pull out of the station. I turned to watch and the sun came out from behind the clouds. The mountains flashed like sugar crystals in the golden light.

Comment

History, the cliche goes, is written by the winners. This is a story not about the losers, but History's castoffs, the people who fought, labored and lost their compatriots in battles no one talks about. We avoid them, sprawled in veterans' hospitals, in cramped shelters and homeless camps. They remind us too much of how easy it is to be caught in some terrible byway of the past, unable to move forward or back. What, I wondered, if there were a way? What would it be? Where would it go?

My dad, before he became an architect, was a reeds man for a number of dance bands around the Midwest in the 40s and 50s. He and others comprised a huge scene, the big bands, that dominated American pop and jazz of that era.. It's gone now, at least in mainstream, commercial media, and had pretty much disappeared while I was growing up.

It amazes and somewhat appalls me, the way our world surges with movements, moments and cultures, only to forget, abandon and supplant them. And of course that process, that fecundity and amnesia, is often anything but innocent. There are many guilty reasons, for instance, why I and many others only found out about the Tulsa race massacre when Watchmen hit the screen.

All of this is a long-winded way of saying that "The Big Rock Candy Mountain" is one of my attempts to resist that obliteration, by trying to inhabit the viewpoint of one of history's forgotten, a homeless doughboy riding the rails, who comes across something strange in his travels.

The End

AT THE SALON

OK, just relax. Let me see, by your chart, you should be a lemon verbena person, right? Oh, don't worry, the facial's included. It's a low-probability lotion, with quantum tunneling conditioners.

So, you still going out with Steve? That's nice - it's good to see people getting along. Who is Steve, these days?

Still doing Kerach - that's been, what, three years? No, I'm just saying, a long time for one avatar. Well that's true - Kerach does suit him, bone structure and personality-wise. How far's he taking it?

Uh huh. Well, you know, this is none of my business, but if I were you, I might tell him to hold off on the prosthetics and make do with the hormones and grafting. My friend told me that GlamTech just got bought by MSoft and you know how they are.

Well, they always say they'll support the backlist, but... Yeah, there's nothing worse than trying to manifest with faulty parts. We had a girl in here - you can't tell anyone, but it was Eloise - and you remember how she had that Gorgon? Tell me about it - every time she needed a tint, one of those damn snakes would bite me. Neurotoxins. And that serum don't come cheap, honey.

Anyway, she was way past warranty. She must have spent most of her credit line getting de-installed. Ball lightning, anaphylactic shock - it was a mess. Plus, she turned my shampoo girl to stone. The lawyers are still talking it over.

OK, now these'll tickle for a bit. Specially bioengineered spider mites. They clean out your pores.

Jerry? Same old same old. You know these cloneboys, always so insecure about identity. He's gotta have every newest thing. This month it's Aldous. Tell me about it. One day you can see right through him, all his organs and everything - that's really great for din-din, let me tell you. The next, he's some kind of superconductor or something - runs around the house, levitating over the toaster, scarin' the cat. The latest is he's getting a job in another dimension.

You think I didn't tell him that? 'Jerry,' I says, 'Jerry, you're barely qualified, not that I'm criticizing, for the job you've got in this dimension. You think they need aura consultants, no matter how cute, in Superstring space? Jerry, it's rough out there - don't get me wrong, but they're liable to send you back as a cloud of Higgs Bosons.' But he's got a friend, see, who's gonna get him in. Supposedly. Guys.

There, doesn't that feel better? Time to put your head back on and we'll start with your somatic re-alignment. Be a doll and reach me that laser-weld, will you?

The End

CUP OF TREMBLING

As she lay paralyzed, save for the occasional spasm, beside the golden body in the middle of the ballroom floor, Miriam admitted privately that she might have made a mistake. The pain was exquisite. It wandered her body like a lover, endlessly finding new corners to fill with sickening shivers, then returning to pulverize familiar nerve endings with fresh agony. She had expected it, though she couldn't have imagined this magnitude of suffering. The old memories hadn't come yet and she'd been promised they'd be worse, far worse. To forestall them for as long as possible she forced her mind back to yesterday afternoon, wondering, now that it was too late, what else she could have done.

* * *

It began, not in innocence--a very scarce commodity in her circle--but uneventfully, at least on the surface. Yet another Buddy Klavan gala, this one in honor of Labor Day, celebrating his return to the capitol and the imminent departure of Washington DC's summer tourists. The only odd thing about it, for those in the know, was that Miriam Hutchins was nowhere in evidence. And Miriam handled Buddy's functions, or at least the ones a prudent journalist could mention.

Miriam had in fact gotten an invitation like some second-stringer, dropped off late by a common courier at the villa in Umbria. She'd been engaged in the pool with Keith, one of her pet Olympic divers when Snuggles started to yammer. Things were coming along very nicely, but somehow Miriam knew whatever had arrived at her door needed attention post haste. Disengaging, she scooped up the Lhasa

Apso and stalked out without a word to Keith. Not bothering to pull on her bathing suit, she strode, a tall, slim, auburn-maned vision of still-dripping aristocracy, into the salon. The maid had seen far worse, after all.

The thing she'd secretly dreaded was on the Louis Quinze sideboard when she arrived, one of the distinctive green-and-gold banded envelopes Buddy had made privately. She paused without touching it, barely registering the putt-putt of a moped receding down the front drive, studying the letter where it lay on the silver Georgian salver as if gauging the mood of a poisonous snake. Her handwritten name on the front was in Buddy's unmistakable forceful scrawl, not the spidery, wavering script of his latest notes. A remission? Or just a previously-signed envelope hoarded against a dire eventuality?

There was only one way to find out. Steeling herself, she set Snuggles down carefully, picked up the letter and broke the seal.

When she'd ascertained that what she was reading were neither her husband's last, dying words, nor the businesslike consolations of his law firm, but an invitation to a party in what he insisted on calling the Georgetown digs, Miriam's painstakingly maintained complexion acquired the delicate pink tinge that warned those who knew her to edge away cautiously.

Calling her emotions mixed would be a severe understatement. "Two weeks," she hissed. "Two weeks and not a word, not a clue about where he's been. All the markers I pulled in, the detectives... How the hell does Buddy Klavan vanish off the face of the earth anyway? And now I find out no, he's not lying in a ditch or kidnapped or dead in some potter's field. No he's back in Georgetown and giving a party! Oh, and gosh I almost forgot, wifey's invited. If you think I'm going to come running, Buddy..."

But as the words trailed off Miriam knew she was going. "Lucrezia!" she bellowed. Snuggles whined, then ran back to the pool.

"Si, Signora?" the maid answered timorously.

"Start packing my bags for the States right now. Make sure you put the blue Givenchy in there. Oh, and the de la Renta, the black and red one. And the Blahnik pumps--owww, shit..." She winced at the familiar stinging cramp. On top of everything, the news would come at this time of the month. "For my sins," she murmured, then set about readying herself to leave.

As soon as the private jet reached cruising altitude Miriam was on the phone again, starting where she'd left off when the limo stopped at the airport. He'd obviously turned his cel phone and answering machine off. Three calls to the Georgetown mansion left her fuming. No one was picking up, no matter how imperious her demands, and some twit had replaced the former discreet outgoing message with a florid invitation to "a real bang-up shivaree" and some strange gabble about "love over tyranny". If anything encapsulated what Buddy Klavan was not about, she reflected, "love over tyranny" was it.

Further phone calls to her network of Beltway insiders yielded no more satisfaction. At first she tried to sound casual, transatlantically bored and looking for a little light gossip, hoping Buddy's doings would come to light. When that didn't work she finally broke down and started asking about him. No one seemed to know anything. Most, she was gratified to find, had no idea Buddy was ill or that he'd disappeared, having accepted, as she'd intended, that he and Miriam had taken their customary solo vacations. The few in the know were just as mystified as she and asked why no one was answering at the mansion.

By this time she was deep in a Pamprin and Daiquiri induced funk, courtesy Rodrigo, the plane's steward and one of Buddy's boys. He knew no more than she, save that Juan-Carlos the upstairs valet had called and left a message saying he was on an extended paid vacation home in Caracas and to drop by sometime. Miriam wondered why Buddy would let him do that now, at the start of the legislative season. Nothing made any sense. She played for a while with Snuggles. She wrote out some extraordinarily generous cheques for PETA and three of her chosen wildlife sanctuaries. She made a few desultory phone maneuvers toward stealing away the guest of honor from another Capitol Hill hostess. It was no good. Nothing made her feel any better.

Finally she decided to phone their Georgetown neighbor, Portia Hargreave. Large of butt, dim of brain and possessing one of the world's most annoying giggles, Portlya, as Miriam termed her, was for some inexplicable reason one of Buddy's favorites. Every so often he'd blow off a meeting with one of his junk bond salesmen or Balkan warlords and Miriam would find them gossiping over tea in the balcony garden. The things he told that little chatterbox had, she was sure, resulted in a few wars when Dictator A got word of the fling Consul B had had with his Bumboy C. Miriam cordially loathed her, not that Portia seemed to notice. But if anyone would know what was up, it was Portia.

While she waited for Portia to pick up Miriam re-read Buddy's note. It was maddeningly uninformative, an ordinary engraved invitation after weeks when nothing was normal, completely standard except for a little note he'd written at the bottom: "Looking forward to sharing a drink, not at the same time, but from the same source. Drink as you have poured." Whatever the hell that meant.

Finally Portia answered. "Miriam, dear!" she burbled. "So good to hear from you! Isn't it amazing about Buddy? He looks wonderful! Two days ago I was sure he'd died of AIDS somewhere." How Portia had survived all these years as the daughter of an oilman, then wife and widow of an investment banker, without learning even elementary discretion was an enduring mystery.

"Portia, you terrible thing." Miriam's smile was a finely honed blade. " I do hope you haven't been going around dropping the "A" word in the wrong ears."

"Oh, you know me." She giggled and Miriam could feel her fingers become talons. Yes, and more's the pity, she thought.

But Portia wasn't finished. "Buddy will be so glad you're coming. He says he and the gardener have been planning this party for three weeks."

Miriam couldn't help herself. "Portia, three weeks ago Buddy was thin as a wraith and in a vegetative coma. And, the gardener? Since when has Esteban become a party consultant?"

"Not Esteban, the new gardener. Ganny-something. Buddy can't stop talking about him. I said 'Buddy, I think you're smitten,' and he smiled and said 'Portia, he saved me.' Like he'd found religion. What do you think of that?"

What Miriam thought was that Buddy had had flings before, though he'd never gone so far as to let his current nancy boy influence his social calendar. Giving Buddy a hetero alibi was in fact the largest part of why they'd married. In return she got unparalleled access and influence in the highest circles of Washington DC.

She got Portia off the line without learning much more, but not screaming in irritation, just as the plane was making its approach to

Dulles. She chewed her lower lip in concentration. Something had changed and she couldn't tell whether she needed to ride it out or jump ship.

It was quite a ship to sail. Everybody who was anybody, or hoped to be somebody, knew Buddy Klavan. Ostensibly he ran a medium sized law and public relations firm with a few select clients. But what Buddy really was, was a fixer. Say a sub-Saharan president's brother had just embezzled half of his country's World Bank loan and needed somewhere to stash it. Through Buddy he'd meet a cheerful, efficient banker from Grand Cayman, a fast-talking Singapore broker with a line on some Panamanian sweatshops and a politely menacing Belgian mercenary contractor who could guarantee round-the-clock protection, should some unpleasantness ensue from his client's peculations. Buddy knew whom to call at Halliburton, how to get a bill rammed through the House, who was looking for landmines and who had them. He had strings to pull in Mossad and Hamas, in the IRA and MI5, among his many other conflicting clients. If you needed to buy a seat in the Senate or just a Senator, Buddy was your man. He was indispensable to those whose choices were gold or the gallows. And now something had changed.

* * *

Two hours later, still somewhat disheveled and thoroughly discomfitted, she sat at the bar in the ballroom, watching Buddy dance with a minor Rothschild princess and wondering what the hell was happening. The events of the last 45 minutes had almost eclipsed those of the last three weeks for maddening strangeness. Sex with Buddy was not unprecedented for her, but rare. He was versatile, but definitely preferred boys. Unprotected sex in the cloakroom with an HIV-positive Buddy, who nevertheless looked better than she'd ever seen before, hypnotically persuasive and masterfully passionate, that was going to take a little sorting out. She'd taken all the post-hoc disease precautions she could and felt her risks were low, though that would have to be monitored. Other things would sort themselves out eventually.

The party was winding down, at least for anybody who mattered. The Cheneys and Rumsfelds had been and gone, the prettier and smarter Bright Young Things had made their connections and left, leaving laggard and unlucky wannabes to chat each other up and work what Buddy called *gli Supplicanti*: the usual mob of arms dealers, junk bond salesmen, also-ran Saudi royalty, lease-hungry oilmen and prowling lobbyists.

The trouble, she reflected, with a Buddy Klavan "do", was that unless she managed to rein it in, people took the nomenclature all too literally. For anyone worth inviting, soirées weren't for *doing*, but for *being*. Being seen, being stroked, being shaken down. Being grateful, most of all, for having been invited.

Right now there were too many heedless nobodies doing things. A group of junior brokers and legislative assistants had broken out a case of Armagnac and were playing some drinking game, giggling like freshmen at a kegger. Others were gyrating wildly to music played too loud for their betters to conduct business. And darting in and among them, like a laughing Lord of Misrule, was Buddy, dancing, filling glasses with better wine than this mob merited, hobnobbing with the orchestra, for God's sake.

It was all too close to out of hand. Celebrating a miraculous recovery was one thing, but Buddy wasting hours of flesh-pressing, deal-making time to dance the limbo with Cher and some boob-jobbed minor countess was quite another. She could see the people he should be talking to, generals, movie producers, industrialists, moneymen, lobbyists, PR reps for cocaine jefes and African warlords. They were gathered on the outskirts of the party, awkward as spurned suitors, sucking their drinks, beginning to get ugly.

She considered trying to get Buddy off the floor again. He'd shrugged her off a few minutes ago, something that hadn't happened in years, something, indeed, that she'd forgotten could happen. Scowling she turned back to the bartender. "Not that champagne - I said the *blanc de noirs*. Christ, watch how you pass it. Spill one drop on my Givenchy and kiss your green card goodbye."

"Sorry, Ms Klavan." His voice had a strange, breathy rasp.

Everyone knew she had kept her maiden name, Hutchins, and abhorred being called Ms. She was about to tear into the ugly new barkeep again when she stopped herself. Abusing the help was bad form. Aside from risking a servant's revenge, she knew from experience that habitual tyrants often made traumatic, indiscreet confessions to the very maid they'd bullied an hour before, doubling their vulnerability. Her momentary lapse in control was due to too many Daiquiris, Pamprin and annoyance at how the party was going. That, she decided, and relief.

Crawling to the Moon, Page 90

Three weeks ago, when Buddy fell into a coma at his annual RPQ picnic she had staged a one-woman cell phone Inquisition of the medical staff at Brydon's clinic, demanding half-hourly updates on his condition, ordering in specialists, raging at their comforting words. She camped out by the bedside, straining to see some sign, any sign that he was coming to. She read to him, though that felt silly. She did Sergeant-at-Arms duty on the cell phone, postponing appointments, stalling interview requests and most of all maintaining the illusion of normalcy by dint of blithe dissembling to those who didn't suspect and icily measured threats to those who did.

When he disappeared she went thermonuclear, reducing Brydon, his head nurse and two orderlies to quivering puddles before concluding that the only piece of intelligence they had was that Buddy had started to look very healthy for a man who'd come in with advanced Kaposi's sarcoma and other fatal complaints.

Then she started working the phones. He hadn't been home to their *pied a terre* in DC, according to Adolfo, the houseboy. At Georgetown Manu told her that nobody had seen him. Later she called every one of their scattered apartments and villas, with no further success. After contacting an expensively discreet detective agency, she was at loose ends. She decided that to maintain the illusion of business as usual she needed to go on her usual solo vacation, leaving her numbers and strict instructions that she was to be contacted if anything turned up. That was two weeks ago.

But enough. As a businesswoman, Miriam Hutchins prided herself on dealing with contingencies quickly and firmly. She despised post-facto rehashing and hand-wringing. It was time to take control.

"When you see the others, tell the upstairs man to start packing it up. And tell him to make sure that stupid emir hasn't passed out in the solarium or the library or someplace."

"Yes, Ms Klavan."

"It's Hutchins, not Klavan. You just call me Ma'am. You're the on ballroom duty for the rest of the night--just be ready to serve till all hours. And get everything cleaned up. Oh, and take that tacky trophy cup down from over the bar."

"Mr. Klavan told me to put it up there, Ma'am."

"Well, I'm telling you to take it down. Where Buddy finds some of these things I'll never know. It looks hideous. And the inscriptions in some made-up language--my old classics teacher would laugh herself silly. Take it away."

"Mr. Klavan asked me to put it back in its case at the end of the evening, Ma'am."

"He's had a case made for the thing too? Honestly, what's he thinking of these days? Buddy's usually such a shrewd investor."

"I wouldn't know, Ma'am."

"No, I don't suppose you would. Buddy looks like he's still got a head of steam on. It's amazing. I haven't seen him dance that way in years. Pour me another."

"Coming up, Ma'am."

"Look at him, groping that Rothschild slut. "

"He's like a new man, isn't he?"

"What the hell would you know about it?"

"Nothing, Ms--Ma'am."

"Shit, we'll have to pay the orchestra double, if it goes any later. Why's he got you tending bar anyway? Buddy always has Armando do these affairs."

"Armando's at Groton now. I said I'd help out."

"Groton, is it? Buddy must have pulled in a few markers for that. The only English Armando knew was "blow job", when he got here. What's your name, anyway?"

"Ganymedo, Ma'am."

"You're not one of the boys. He likes them bigger and younger."

"No, Ma'am."

"Wait a minute. You're that new gardener Buddy was so excited about. I've never seen him so--Oh, hello, Senator."

"'Something strange going on here."

"What would that be, Jerry?"

"C'mon, Miriam, don't kid a kidder. Ever since Buddy--look at him, dancing with Cher. Seems like all he wants to do is dance. Now, I understand, new lease on life and everything. But business is business. We had those trade bill riders all set up a couple of months ago. The antipersonnel mine exemption package. Get the veepee to sign off and ba-boom, right up the middle. 'Stead, Buddy's puttin' me off. Wants to tango with Cher and what's-her-face, that princess with the hooters. I mean, this is Buddy we're talking about."

"I know, Jerry. I'll talk to him."

"What the hell happened to him, anyway? Last time I saw him at RPQ here, he looked pale and shaky. Nobody said anything: If Buddy wants to call it 'a touch of the flu' and George and Dick back him up, then that's what it is. But everybody's glad he don't wanna get down in the bushes and join the fun, if you catch my drift. Anyway, next thing I hear, Buddy's dying."

"I understand there was a pool on whether he'd make it till the Senate recessed."

"Well, you know Frank and Oren and that crowd. Those bitches have no taste. I'm sorry you heard about it."

"I'm a big girl, Jerry. Everybody copes however they can."

"Jus' the same, I was glad to see Frank didn't get elected, this time around. Serves him right.

"You're a true friend, Jerry. As soon as we get this mob on their way, I'll have Buddy set up your bill."

"I'd appreciate it. Well, anyway, time to pack it in. Flight to Rio in the morning."

"Make sure you spend some time at our beach house. You look like you could use it."

"If only I could. I'll be holed up with some beaner generales who wanna trade tortillas for armoured personnel carriers. Christ, sometimes I think I should have stayed in the Senate. Pay was terrible and the hours were bad, but at least they weren't always breathing chilis in your face."

"Just the same, I'll tell Feliz to look for you."

"Thanks, Miriam, you're a peach. So long."

"Uh, Ma'am, Mr. Klavan had the beach house closed up last week. I understand he found Feliz a job with the Canadian Trade Mission."

"OK, what is going on here? Buddy loves that house. He would never let it go. And speaking of that, where are the rest of the boys? And who the hell are you, anyway?"

"Tell you what, Miriam. You fill me up a plate from the buffet table and I'll tell you what I know."

"Just who do you think you're talking to, you little dago? I asked you a direct question and I want an answer."

"Well, maybe I should let Mr. Klavan explain."

"Look, Ganymedo, maybe you don't understand how things stand here. This is Washington D.C., la capital de los Estados Unidos, comprende?

"Yes Ma'am."

"Good. And in Washington D.C., Mr. R. H. Klavan is at the top of his field, a *jefe*, a big man. This means when Buddy gives a party, everybody who's anybody comes and you aren't anybody if you're not invited. And I organize his parties. Got that?"

"Yes, Ma'am. Mr. Klavan speaks of you often."

"Oh, so now you're telling me you know who Mr. Klavan speaks of 'often'. I don't think I'm getting through to you, Ganymedo, and for your sake you'd better catch on quick. I don't care what goes down in San Taco or wherever you come from: My relationship with Buddy is business. We're partners. So don't give me that lopsided smile, like I'm some rich man's *chiquita*. There's something weird happening here and you're part of it. What part I'm going to find out, right now."

"I really think you ought to ask Mr. Klavan about that, Ma'am."

"Fine. I'll just go and--Where'd he go?"

"He was heading upstairs with the princess last time I saw him."

"Goddammit, what is this? First me and now that Rothschild tootsie? The last thing I thought I'd have to worry about is Buddy turning into Henry Kissinger. Oop--Sorry, Hank. So good of you to come. Drop in any time."

"Not entirely, Ms Klavan. Mr. Klavan is just more, as you said, 'versatile'. He had quite an extended leave-taking with Armando last week. 'Linking by love', I think is his phrase for it. He's talking about setting up a charitable foundation, too."

"So that's what he was on about, all the time in the den. Hard to make out words when they're being tongued into your ear. My God, he was so... and without any protection, either... What kind of foundation? This isn't that 'Love Over Tyranny' nonsense he was on about, is it?"

"I believe so, yes."

"Christ, Buddy's had wild ideas before, but this time he's gone off the deep end. What the hell has he--"

"Could you fill me up that plate from the buffet table now, Miriam?"

"All right, Mister, I'll just do that thing. I have to go see people out anyway, at least before that Iraqi general drowns himself in the punch bowl. But you better have some answers when I get back."

* * *

"There you are, have some of these. They've got truffles in them. You have to at least pretend to like them, if you want to move in these circles. Pour me another."

"Here you go. I do like truffles, as it happens. I used to supply them to the King of Burgundy."

"Ganymedo, let me correct a misconception: Not every Americano is completely obtuse about history or geography. There is no King of Burgundy."

"An old and distinguished line, long since extinct."

"On the other hand, it's an apt image: following a pig on a leash and grubbing in the dirt for some pathetic pretender to an archaic throne. Kind of sums things up, doesn't it?"

"If you like."

"So you're French, then."

"Not especially."

"I didn't think you looked Latino, really. You don't look like anything, actually, except bent up and strange. Have you got some kind of disease? What kind of name is Ganymedo, anyway?"

"No to the one, an inadequate translation to the other."

"Wait a minute--Ganymedo, Ganymede--cup bearer to the Gods.

"At your service."

"Boy, your parents sure saddled you with a howler. Wasn't he supposed to be beautiful? Beloved of Zeus, something like that?"

"In some stories, yes. The later ones."

"The least Buddy ought to do is get you some dental work, if he's going to keep you around. I've never seen such a set of snaggle teeth."

"He's offered. Braces don't work very well on me, I'm afraid."

"Which brings us around to the main question: Who the hell are you and what are you doing here?"

"I'm what you thought I was: I'm a gardener. At least that's the only work I'm really trained for. I work for Mr. Klavan. For now."

"No, I don't think so. You're not his type--too homely by half. Let's see . . . I've got it--You're from one of his coke connections.

Yes, that's it. You've got a weird Indio look about you--some kind of Columbian tribesman, maybe? Got any freebies behind the bar?"

"No samples."

"Everybody gives tastes around here, Mr. Big Supplier. What are you, an in-law from some Cali family, looking for a leg up in Anglo society? Can you get me an uncut ounce?"

"I've got medicine for what ails you. Look at Buddy."

"He does seem better these days.

"Particularly for someone who was on his deathbed a few weeks ago."

"Who told you that? You're not from People or something, are you?"

"News travels. And no, I'm not a reporter. Buddy and I have an acquaintance that is recent, but intense. I put him in touch with his... misgivings."

"Buddy--doubts? Not likely. Are you some kind of hustling evangelist? Boy, that'd be a twisted joke, even for him."

"Am I going to try and get you to fall to your knees and pray for your immortal soul, while I peek down your neckline? Sorry. My business is with your husband and it's of a different order. I'm honored to have put him out of business."

"You? Fat chance. You saw them crowding around him. People who could buy and sell you twenty times out of pocket change. And it's always the same: Buddy could you fix this, Buddy could you arrange that. He was dealing before you came in and he'll be dealing when you're gone. Where does a jerk in a borrowed Armani suit get off talking like he's shut Buddy Klavan down?"

"A lot of those people are going to be very disappointed. Buddy can still do a lot of favors, but he's picked up a bad case of something he never had before--scruples."

"My husband is a very principled person!"

"The only principal any of these people recognize is the one whose interest they live off of."

" There's nothing worse than lefty snobs. Look, over there-- there's Al Gore. You can't get a lot more liberal and honest than that. And he's a close friend of Buddy's."

"First I'm a mountebank, then a dealer--now I'm a Marxist? I think what you're trying to call me is a poor person, my dear. And of course all these people are 'close friends' of your husband. Even if they hate him and will spend tomorrow thinking of ways to take him down. Because they may need him someday. And because Nature may abhor a vacuum, but politics demands one."

"Listen, you--"

"This is all very pleasant, Miriam, but before we get into it, would you like another drink?"

"Out of that? I'd sooner drink from a toilet bowl." The cup he'd brought down from the shelf over the bar was not just dirty looking. It seemed somehow to be made of soil, if you looked at right. At other angles it seemed like some strange, primitively cast metal. Or stoneware. Or leather. It was definitely odd and the symbols around the rim looked like nothing she'd ever seen.

"See the inscription around the rim? In Sumerian it means something like 'Drink As You Have Poured'."

"Is that supposed to mean something to me?"

"Pass me the wine, please. A nice Chambertin, perfect."

"OK, so it holds wine, big deal. You mind keeping it steady? That's an antique mahogany sideboard you've got it over."

"Why don't you hold it?" He passed it to her.

"Is this a gag? Why is it shaking?"

"Try to stop it."

"I can't!"

"That, Little Ms Plutocrat, is the only, original Cup of Trembling. Isaiah mentions it: 'Behold, I have taken out of thine hand the cup of trembling, even the dregs of the cup of my fury', as does Zechariah. But even then the secret of it had been long lost and the Hebrews thought of it as a political metaphor, not an actual thing. This is the real deal, das *Ding an sich*, the Cup in which Mother Inanna held the sacred Me. The ur-Vessel of Life. Beside it, the Holy Grail is a Dixie Cup."

"I can't hold it much longer! What happens if I set it down?"

"Nothing, if you do it carefully. Try not to spill it--that could be rather, um, unpleasant."

"There. Jesus. Alright, assuming, just for the moment, that this thing is not a hoax--that it doesn't have a motor or something in the base--what's this got to do with Buddy?"

"How do your hands feel, now that you've gripped the Cup?"

"Weird, now that you mention it. They hurt, but somehow they feel... strong."

Crawling to the Moon, Page 97

"The Cup has two virtues. It can confer life and strength to those who hold and drink from it."

"Like, um, Eternal Life?"

"I leave that to preachers. But more life than before."

"I can't believe this. I'm standing here talking with some seedy little bottom feeder about a cup that makes magic potions."

"Fine, go chat with one of those young investment bankers. Look, there's one headed our way."

"Oh shit. Hi, Jimpie."

"Hello, Miriam. A bunch of us are heading over to Chazzie's for a few lines. Like a lift?"

"No, I'm going to stay and grow a taproot. Catch you later."

"Erm, well, fine. Well, see you, then..."

"Not your sort of *Uebermensch*?"

"Doing coke with that crowd is like being embalmed, only you have to make small talk while it happens."

"Whereas I, while a nutbar, am at least interesting."

"No, you're just a nobody I can blow off. Bye now."

"Your husband is an amazing specimen. Not many men his age can limbo, especially since he was nearly dead three weeks ago. Could he have done that before, I wonder?"

"What are you saying?"

"Oh, nothing. Care to drink from the Cup?"

"OK... I'll bite. Tell me how your piece of junkshop tin saved my husband."

"Well, first I thought it had done anything but. I met him at his annual RPQ garden party."

"RPQ?"

"Don't be coy, Ms Warbucks - it doesn't suit you. Rich and Powerful Queens. The Closet of the Gods. Where J. Edgar Hoover used to make smoochie with Cardinal Spellman. This affair, since Buddy was hosting, had more of a 'youth' theme than was perhaps usual. Twelve-year-olds in lederhosen, if I remember correctly."

"OK, no more insinuations. You're just lucky nobody in his firm can hear you. My husband cares for homeless boys out of the goodness of his heart. And I'm sick of little creepos like you spreading smutty rumours. I mean, look at these people. Royalty, politicians, stars--all world-class paparazzi bait. They're on guard against scandal every day, because they have to be. Do you think they'd associate with a child molester?"

"Oh, come now. What you, your husband and everyone here has understood from back when you discovered that Nursie was afraid of you, afraid you'd send her back to Guatemala or wherever--is what you can do with power. And one thing money and clout does is keep *de facto*, what everybody knows, and *de jure*, what anyone can say, a long way apart. As long as Buddy never admits it, and nobody says or writes it--it didn't happen. How many publishers and network heads are here? And they all owe him something. With friends like these, your husband could eat human flesh from living victims and no one would know, not really. How many parties have you been to here, with more pretty boys than you could shake a stick at?"

"I don't see any here now. What I see is Buddy dancing up a storm with Cher."

"Isn't he though? But you're right - he sent young Gary and Piero off to boarding school the other day. Have to make do with adults, I guess."

"I can't believe what a prig you are. What are you, Jerry Falwell's secret agent? Do you actually believe you've 'cured' my husband?"

"Jerry is one of Buddy's biggest clients, as I'm sure you know. And I cured nothing. That was the Cup."

"Oh yeah, the famous Cup. How, pray tell, did it do that?"

"I managed to get Buddy alone in his garden and explain how it worked. It was easier than I thought it would be. He'd been feeling sick for months. You must have noticed."

"Just a little pale, is all."

"Yes, well, your pale husband had just had the bad news he expected at a checkup. He was desperate. Kaposi's."

"Jesus, this gets more and more incredible. Go on."

"Well, I filled it up with what he had with him--Diet Pepsi--and he drank it down. We were in one of those nooks in his topiary maze, out there in the back--near the fountain? It was two a.m. or so. All around, I could hear Washington power brokers putting their deals across, as it were. And Buddy was choking and thrashing on his manicured lawn, his hair falling out as he smashed his head on the ground. Then he went into a coma."

"Just assuming, for the sake of argument, that something happened at one of Buddy's parties. How would a little bottom feeder like you get in? He keeps security tight."

"If it's so tight, why am I here?"

"You--"

"All the time we've been talking, have you seen anyone look at me? At either of us?"

"Right, you've got a magic cup and you're invisible. If I grab you will you lead me to a pot of gold?"

"Not invisible, just nondescript. Being the Cup Bearer, well, let's just say it allows you to pick your spots. You can kind of keep things vague in your vicinity. People look, they just don't see if you don't want them to. Of course with this crowd it's easy. They see someone emptying a trashcan or holding a tray and their eyes just bounce right off. It was harder at the clinic. Doctors and med staff are pretty observant. And they've got all those surveillance cameras these days. But we pulled it off."

"OK, while we're in fantasy-land, where did he go?"

"Here, of course. It's a lot more comfortable than any clinic."

"You couldn't have come here. One of the boys would have called me."

"They never knew, until we started changing things. As I said, vague. It's pretty easy in a house as big as this."

"But why? And why didn't anyone tell me?"

"Aye, there's the rub, isn't it? Why was the Queen of Insiders left on the Outside? The truth is Buddy needed time to fully recover. And to plan this party. That's the first thing he said to me when I got into his room at the clinic to give him a second drink from the Cup. 'I want you to help me with a party.'"

"Buddy Klavan can plan his own parties, thank you very much."

"But this one's special. It's the one where he's letting people know, in his own way, that he's not in the mayhem for money business any more. Those two gents trying to catch his eye? General Khalid has personally tortured and killed thousands. He wants Buddy to get him back on the State Department dole. Bruster Carlyle's family owns garment sweatshops all over the country, pays starvation wages to immigrant women and murders union organizers. They're just two of many who depend on Buddy to help them out when they need good publicity or loopholes. They'll leave if they don't get what they need. And after a while they won't come back. Don't you look at me like that, you empty-headed, nose-jobbed little leech--you know it's true."

"Hey, fuck you. I don't have to take this. I'm calling security."

"Go right ahead, if you think it'll do any good. But clear it with your husband. Because it's a party for me too."

"What have you got to celebrate?"

"Tonight I drink from the Cup again. For the last time, I hope."

"If it's really the cure-all you make it out to be, why would you stop using it?"

"I'm old, Miriam. Older than any man should be. This hasn't been my world for thousands of years. But I keep drinking from the Cup. Sooner or later, it has to kill me." He smiled, crookedly. "But that's what I thought the last time I drank. And here I am."

"And you're telling me all this because..."

"I want to pass it on."

"So if you die and I drink, then I become the new Cup Bearer. Is that how it works?"

"Pretty much, I think. Truthfully, I'm not really sure. I don't have much in the way of precedent."

"Would I be as ugly as you?"

"You don't get very tall if you grow up living on what you can grow in the furrows your bronze plough makes behind your ox. Armani suits aren't made for bandy, peasant legs and broad shoulders. When you've lost your teeth and regrown them so many times you've lost count, they don't come in straight any more. When every bone in your body has been smashed and healed, with or without a splint, you tend to look a little odd. Of course, I haven't drunk from the Cup in a while." He smiled again and shrugged his massive, uneven shoulders. "I think though, if you take care of yourself, with present-day health care methods you should be a hottie for a long, long time."

"Why me?"

"You're young, strong, even stronger than Buddy. You've got connections and brains. And you're sick."

"I most certainly am not. My last checkup--You mean from when Buddy and I--You can't know that! I'm not--"

"Relax, Miriam. You're clean, at least physically. Really, you're fine. What I mean is you can't stand your own species. How humanity makes you soul-sick. Buddy's told me about Snuggles, how she's really your only friend. About the big donations to PETA. How you've got it in for Lydia von Coburg. Why would that be, I wonder?"

"She's in the pet of the month club. She's always got the latest. When Shar Peis were in she had a matched pair. She had a Pyrenees Mastiff after that stupid movie came out. I hear she's trying to get an Africanis to take to that African Relief Benefit next month. And they all end up in the pound when she's through with them."

"So torturers, drug dealers, all the purveyors of human misery Buddy and you deal with, they don't bother you. But let somebody give a doggie the toss..."

"Shut up. This Cup--Will it send me off the deep end, like Buddy?"

"Ah. Well, the Cup of Trembling changes people. Zoroaster was a pretty run-of-the-mill guy before he had drink from the Cup. Saint Stephen would have gone on being a Legionary, and a pretty nasty piece of work too, if he hadn't."

"So it'll make me into a saint or a prophet?"

"Not necessarily. I wouldn't call Lorenzo de Medici a saint. Nor Hamurabi or Catherine the Great. More like people who suddenly saw what needed to be done and could do it. Now Marcus Aurelius, he was sort of a saint, a dull one..."

"I don't believe this. You're telling me that every single major figure in history has drunk from this Cup."

"Of course not. But lots did."

"Queen Elizabeth the First? "

"Sure. She drank some mulled cider."

"Joan of Arc?"

"She was just crazy."

"King Solomon?"

"Check."

"Jesus, that's... What about Jesus?"

"Jesus." He frowned. "Jesus was a mistake."

"He shouldn't have drunk from it? Why not?"

"He never did. That was Mary. Those stories about what a Goodie Two-Shoes she was, what a crock. I was in a caravan with them. I wasn't going to Bethlehem either. That was just where they holed up a few nights later. Joseph wasn't the quickest bunny in the forest, but a good sort. She was trouble. About to pop any day and it didn't even slow her down. Way too interested in other people's business and sticky fingers, I found out. I got a bit snockered one night and woke up to find her going through my things. Before I could stop her or say anything she'd poured the rest of my wine into the Cup and gulped it down. Maybe the stupid wench had cravings."

"What happened to her?"

"She gasped, like someone had kicked her in the stomach, then staggered back to her own tent. You never can tell, with the Cup. Sometimes they walk away under their own steam or they lie there for days. Sometimes they go mad or it kills them flat out."

"Can you tell? Can you tell if you're going to get through it?"

"Well, there is a sensation. It's kind of a sharp little pain, then it feels like there's a pressure release in places you never knew you had. Marie Curie told me it was like the ping! she felt at ovulation. Some women say they can feel that exact moment."

"So what really happened with Mary? After that?"

"Oh, I left the caravan and tried not to give it a second thought. I didn't hear anything about her and I assumed that she'd died or gone mad. Or maybe nothing had changed. Sometimes the Cup doesn't change anything. Thirty odd years later, I saw Him and I knew right away. What a load of trouble that was."

"Has that kind of thing ever happened to you any other time?"

"With Guatama Buddha. But I don't want to talk about that."

"So this thing can make me a Great Woman, just by drinking from it. What's the catch, Ganymedo?"

"Isn't pain and possible madness or death catch enough?

"That's a catch, but it isn't all there is. You're holding out on me, I can tell."

"Miriam, Miriam..." He grinned, his dark, cockeyed face looking strangely boyish. "I'm almost beginning to like you. The catch." He swung the cup out toward the dark ballroom, bracing against the trembling in his hand. The party had died around them. All the Bright Young Things, all the Movers and Shakers had left. The orchestra had packed and gone. The tables were moved to one side. Crepe decorations drooped and waved gently in a faint breeze. Even Buddy had gone to bed. "The catch is that you'll never see the world the same way again. It will be like this, dark and alone."

He drank deeply from the Cup, staring into her eyes. He winced, but seemed to be taller, suddenly. "The catch is that you might gain years of health, possibly wisdom, perhaps greatness, but at a cost. And that cost is personally suffering, really feeling, all at once, all the pain and degradation, not just that you've caused personally, but that you've made possible." He set the Cup down carefully and ran a hand that looked straighter, more supple, over the strange writing around the rim. "'Drink As You Have Poured'. The Cup of Trembling. The Cup of Wrath."

"Who sent you here with your spiel and magic tricks? This is sick."

"Not as sick as Buddy was. Think of it--all that agony--the shrieking pain of bullets slamming into your guts and heart, the slow, clamping ache of starvation, the small shocks of hurt as you limp down the street on twisted legs, the cold strangulation of unending fear, the bewilderment and shame as your anus is ratcheted open by the only man who ever showed you any kindness. Every class of torment, all together, for as long as the Cup's draught is in your body. Many others have died or gone mad--George the Third, Attila, Hitler. To name a few." He shook his head and misshapen yellow teeth spilled out of his mouth. She could see straight, white ones pushing up out of his gums as he talked. She felt like she was going crazy.

"None of this can be true."

"They lay there, sick unto death, for days or weeks. Because that's what happens when you bring de facto and de jure together at last. The Cup puts the color back into deals signed in black and white or in invisible whispers--the colour of shit, of blood." He stared at her with piercing dark eyes, the whites so clear they were bluish. "Others came through like Buddy. They opened their eyes and recovered, more than recovered, feeling better than they ever had. They went on to become wise and compassionate leaders--Ashoka, Kublai Khan, Roosevelt--and lived longer than their allotted spans, for as long as they had the Cup. As long as they drank deep of the pain which was their legacy." His voice was the baritone thunder of a strong young man. Suddenly he shrieked, a hoarse, grinding sound. He fell then, hard and without catching himself, lying like a golden statue of a beautiful peasant boy. His nose started to bleed.

"My God, who let you in, you little madman?"

"The memories," he gritted through a clenched grin. "The memories are the worst part. How about it, Miriam? Once the Cup has been filled, someone has to drink it dry. I'm used to it - it won't do any more for me. But you, well, you've only got a few marks against you. So far. The fat girl you and your friends snubbed and mocked in the dormitory. The servants and underlings you've bullied. All the small mass of people you've humiliated by just being who you are. Or maybe you've done worse, much worse, already. I wouldn't know." Talking seemed to be difficult for him and he gasped sometimes between words. "But you'll go on, from triumph to triumph, sin to sin. You'll be more and more mired in cruelty as you age. You're already older than your years. Because you're ambitious, aren't you? Born to rule and like that."

"I've got to think about this."

"Don't take too long. The Cup moves on quickly. You may not have another chance. Oh, and look--is that a gray hair I see?" His voice was a thin, snarling whisper. Abruptly he spasmed and lay as if paralysed. Only his eyes moved.

Miriam looked down at the still, golden body. "You know," she said, "I've decided to give it a try, just on spec. Might be a giggle." She smiled, looking into his eyes. "But first I want to tell you about something that happened to me this morning. It was a little, sharp ping!, right down here." She pointed to her lower belly. "So we'll see what happens in, say, thirty-odd years." Then she picked up the Cup and drank it dry.

Comment

One of the silliest and most satisfying conventions in any melodrama/thriller, be it Bond movie or superhero comic, is the villain's monologue, where he or she justifies, exults over and explains the horrible things they've put in motion. The worst people, the Mussolinis, Putins and Karla Homolkas of this world never take ownership of their depredations. In the rare cases where they are brought to some kind of reckoning and questioned closely, they always maintain, all evidence to the contrary, that they are victims of misunderstanding and heroes of their own stories.

It's no idle claim. When Ted Bundy, caught dead to rights, would only confess in the form of a rambling, hypothetical, third-person narrative, when Hitler refused to tour bombed-out German cities or look at his country's war victims, they were acting out an overwhelming psychic imperative, the urge to see themselves as innocent, an impulse as strong, maybe stronger, among the most vile and depraved as it is for anyone else.

And really, how could it be any other way? Such people's ability to cause pain far exceeds any one person's capacity to suffer for the harm they've caused. In fact, assuming an ability to quantify hurt, there could be a law stating that the ability to wound others varies inversely, to the square of the perpetrator's empathetic ability. Which is why Leona Helmsley, Dick Cheney and Idi Amin have, all put together, the emotional depth of your average alligator.

Or maybe this is all just cherry-picking. After all, Abraham Lincoln, Mahatma Ghandi and Ho Chi Minh all caused enormous suffering and death in the service of causes most of us would regard as noble. Lyndon Johnson, to what seems to me his enormous credit, made sure that he heard regular, unvarnished accounts from GIs who carried out his orders, never sparing himself from hearing about their pain, fear and loneliness. He still shattered families on both sides for generations with gunfire, Agent Orange, bombing and landmines.

What I'm groping clumsily around is what every major religion promises: perfect, personal Justice. It's an abstraction found nowhere in Nature, which abounds in babies born with incomprehensibly painful genetic anomalies, parasites of parasites of parasites, random death and inescapable decay and degradation. And we want it desperately, to the point where people will deny themselves benefits if they think someone else might be profiting unduly from them. We build vast institutions and put forth monumental energies in the service of this notion which, we acknowledge, can only be distantly approached and varies from age to age and according to your viewpoint.

I've spent a ridiculous amount of time imagining, carefully measuring out and refining the punishments I'd mete out to the powerful few, capricious, cruel, heedless and utterly untouchable, the Trumps, Bushes, Cheneys and Kissingers of this world. But what if there was a better way?

"Cup of Trembling" imagines a way around all that.

The End

BLIND MAN'S WINK

"To die badly is to live badly."

At 170 klicks an hour slewing around boulders, the Citroen's hydraulics gasping and moaning, Ida and Desmond raving half out the back windows, throwing whatever they can at a carload of Moroccan bandits tailgating us, trying to run us off the Berber mountain road that bucks and twists like a wild thing. The sun is going down, we're nowhere near Ketama, running on empty and all I can think about is the last time I saw France and something Paolo mumbled with a head full of gasoline fumes.

We had just finished topping off the tank in Nice, siphoning a BMW dry at 3 in the morning. It was too late for construction, not that I'd ever get into Gibraltar again, and too early for grape-picking. Paolo wanted to head up to Rotterdam, said his lover had a good job waiting for him up there, *tres chouette*. The last time it was Delft. It was a crock anyway, he just wanted to score some China White, sit around smoking with all his mook friends.

If Paolo had any real friends. It was hard to see him connected to anyone, anything. Sometimes I thought that Paolos were made, not born, that any time a gap between races, languages, and desires gaped open, any time people shifted because of markets or madness, somewhere a Paolo was created, a human marker for absence. He said he was Australian and it might even have been true. English was certainly one of the languages he'd lost, dropping out of his mouth like teeth. He talked in a Paolo patois, odd bits of French, German, English, Hindi and Arabic, scunged up against Spanish, what he said was Laotian, Christ knows what else.

He sat in the Vauxhall gumming an apple to kill the fumes, looking up and down the road and said "To die badly is to live badly."

Or something like that, I think. It wasn't like he was talking to me, more like something he'd just realized.

Then he turned and threw me the Blindman's Wink. You know that drinking game where one of you draws the short straw? He's the Blindman, but he keeps it to himself. Sometime while you're all talking, he catches someone's eye and tries to give them a tiny wink while nobody else is watching. If no one else sees it, a little while later that person says "I'm dead", and stops talking. It goes until somebody catches the Blindman in the act or he kills everyone.

We'd play it for hours, the whole squat, mostly weekend junkies, working black at factories and restaurants or turning tricks. It was like being in a house of ghosts, except for that acetone smell you get off malnutrition.

It's getting dark, the mountains are bending over the road, losing that electric green glow that tells you that you are in the hills of the Rif. Ida has shuddered herself down to a huddle of terror. Desmond is not even swearing in *Suissedeutsche* any more, just watching me fight the gearshift, the Mercedes drawing closer, the gold-edged grins, the many arms gesturing, Kali with a straight-6. He looks tired, Desmond does, ready, regretful: an old man checking into a rest home.

I'm a fool getting involved with these two, this run up to Ketama, happy-hippie-hash valley. A hundred and fifty bucks between us to buy a dope stake. Pas de problem to quadruple that. Sell to Americans, Germans. If we can get into town alive. Or out of it.

Brain-dead phantoms crowd the roadside, in among the 9 year olds and grannies with fists full of hash, fer fuckin' shurr they mumble, it's never the trip you thought it was... you never really have your hands on the wheel... we get picked up by this old boy just out of Tonganoxie, we're going to Atlanta and he's heading over to Charleston.

He turns out to be a just divorced, ex-stock car racer, ex-rodeo bronc rider, ex-steel guitar player, Ku Klux Klan Grand Dragon, with a car full of automatic weapons, a radio beeper to let the local cops know that Klan was coming through and never you mind how fast, sippin' sour mash and cruising at 120 behind at least one gorilla biscuit, all your worst Country and Western fantasies come to life...

he likes us, Jan and me, we're not out there miscegenating, but he's getting a tad exercised because of the filling stations, they're all self-service, he want someone to fill the tank for him, why not? It's a goddam deVille, no shame in that... I finally convince him to stop and let me fill her up, but he won't let go of the wheel or give me the keys to get the packs out of the trunk and when he finally lets us out, way off course in Mississippi, my stomach doesn't come unclenched for two days.

I manage to put a little space between us and the Mercedes. The Citroen is a little faster and it's got more torque uphill. It isn't much, but it compensates for my terror and inexperience with this road. The only thing is, we're coming onto a downhill patch. And the road is getting wider...

Ida points to lights through the small gap in the hills - "Ketama!"

"Where's the cop shop?" I scream at Desmond, the only one of us who's been this way before. The Mercedes is edging closer on the right. I can see them passing a *sipsi* back and forth, puffing away on kif. This is home entertainment for these guys. Desmond stares at me. "*Quoi?*"

"The cops! Fuck - the *Surete, les flics*!"

The Mercedes clips us and the Citroen screams and slews like a gaffed tuna. My head hits the windshield. I yank the wheel over and force them into the stone edge of the road. I can see the sparks shrieking out of their side panels before they put on the brakes. They start up again, worse luck.

Desmond is laughing, a crazed, pitiless howl. "There's no police in Ketama! It's just a hotel and some shops!"

He finally sobers up.

"Turn in here."

I do and we go jouncing down a narrow brick road, dodging through a mob of little white-washed houses, ending up in the parking lot of what looks for all the world like a Best Western Motel stuck in the middle of the Rif Mountains. The Mercedes is roaring on our tail.

Desmond pulls out a huge drop knife, opens his door and hits the ground rolling. He's on his feet quick and pounding on the door with the pigsticker's butt. As soon as I can get the car stopped, Ida and I stumble after him, me fumbling in the moneybag under my arm for the stiletto I picked up in Ceuta. I get it out as the Mercedes pulls up.

Crawling to the Moon, Page 109

Out pour 8 or 9 Moroccan versions of Superfly. They've got the wide-brimmed fedoras, they've got the stacked heels, the cream linen baggies, the wescotts with the tricky pockets, the button flies, the permed 'fros, the righteous Raybans. We're caught in some North African Blaxploitation film. I am dangerously close to gibbering.

They're really looped, laughing and trading high fives like a bunch of budget Shafts.

"Hey some ride, peoples, no shit. How come you don't stop? You make big joke, eh?

Ida pulls out her own knife.

"It's no joke!" she grits out.

They crack up and turn towards each other in a little circle, sniggering, trading dance steps and complex handshakes, every now and then exploding in laughter when one of them looks over his shoulder and catches sight of our feckless, exhausted faces.

Finally the hotel owner, a big man in old-fashioned baggy horseman's trousers, opens up. He roars at them in furious Berber and they turn to leave, still laughing. As the car starts up one guy darts out and up to me, holding a fist size lump of Sputnik, the best grade of hash. "

"To show that we are friends." He thrusts it into my hand.

He turns again to go, but not before he's given me a quick sidelong wink.

The End

HEROINE BEER

So, like, I was going for munchies and that, you know, just before the ballgame and the wife's cleaning up the empties from last night and vacuuming and stuff. And she's, "Get some of that Heroine Beer."

I'm, "What? Can't hear you, 'counta the vacuum."

"That Heroine Beer, you know, with like Wonderwoman and Helen Keller on the label."

So, I'm, "Yeah, dope, whatever."

And I get to the store and there's like ten zillion guys with like the same idea as me. And they're all out of my brand - Blond, Hearty Construction Worker Beer and even Cowboys in Pickups Lite. I gotta get a case of Urban Sophisticates in Turtlenecks Ice Filtered, which tastes like piss. But it's either that or Football Hooligan Lager. And I'm about to get in line and wait.

Then I remember - the Heroine Beer. The hell is it? And I'm like, reading all the labels – Semiotician Stout, Happy Brown People Lembic, Peyote Party Pilsner, Social Democratic Vegan Porter, like a kajillion brands. I figure, the fuck with it. And then I see it, the Heroin Beer. Babe on the label looks more like Courtney than Wonderwoman, but whatever.

It's already into the first inning. So I get home and toss the old lady one of her brewskis. She pops it and chugs. And she gets real quiet, which is like, cool, 'cause most of time she keeps wanting to have like relationship talk when I'm trying to watch the game. Then she gets up and ralphs all over the TV.

I'm, "Is that ever totally fucked, man. I mean, I missed a double play and everything."

And she nods off right there and then, on the sofa. So now, everything smells bad, the wife is sawing logs, the screen is going funny, there's some, like, smoke coming out the back of the set, which we haven't paid off yet. And I'm getting low on my beer...

The End

ALL YOUR FEARS ARE FOOLISH FANCY

Come to me, my melancholy baby,
Cuddle up and don't be blue.

One hand still holding his clarinet, Gus is lying on his bed, pulling and stroking himself absently, wishing he had a nickel for a Lemon Coke, when Dorothea starts to sing.

It's near to sunset in August, 1943. The long light is a green gold ember through the buckeye tree outside his window and his aunt's gone to her Sunday canasta game with the Kravetskys across the street. He's done the chores, practised his scales and is warm and drowsy from one of the special cigarettes he smokes for his asthma. He can hear the slight slur to Dorothea's singing. He imagines the Old Gold filter tip she'll have dangling down, stained with the plum-coloured lipstick his aunt says doesn't go with her red hair.

On Dorothea's side of the row house's shared wall, the mate to his room is an upstairs parlour, where she plays a spinet piano, haltingly accompanying herself. That's what she calls it, a parlour, though his aunt says it's nothing but a room turned into a closet, where Dorothea's sisters throw their junk.

His room has the same pink carnation on green wallpaper, but he's covered most of it with publicity shots of Ellington and the Dorseys, with Life Magazine photos of the War, especially of the First Infantry, his brother Jimmy's battalion. On his dresser there's a group shot of Jimmy's graduating class at Officer Training School. Jimmy's at the front, in dress uniform, standing proud and cocky.

There's been a heat wave for three weeks, the Stillwater is down low on the levee and he can almost taste a Lemon Coke, sweet and sharp, or even a shandy like Jimmy mixed him the other day. His throat still feels lined with creek stones from the asthma fit half an hour ago, but the pain is muted, sunken into his body's quiet resonances. Even the pinging throb in his temples is a grace note, as if he were a heavy, warm cloud, calmly absorbing itself in its own sweeps and rhythms, slowly permeating everything. Arousal is a distant, steady shock, only his because it seems vaguely as if it must belong to someone.

Dorothea's playing is awkward today, as if the song overwhelmed her usually agile fingers, her right hand a little girl in Mother's high heels, left clumping heavily, like it's wearing a polio brace, trying to catch up. She keeps hitting the dead key she usually chords around.

He likes playing with her: She can really read music. They do tunes like "I'm Always Chasing Rainbows" and "Perdido" together. Her piano's against the wall they share, jammed in among horsehair furniture, old gowns, a birdcage like a Turkish Palace, her collection of ivory and tortoiseshell combs and, over in the corner, a huge wickerwork baby carriage.

She sometimes calls him Gussie, like when his father, Big Gus, was alive and when he tells her no, my name is Gus now, she tousles his red hair and calls him her little boy.

A year ago, before he grew three inches, he climbed into the big basket-weave stroller and yelled boo when she came into the room. She jumped back, nearly fell downstairs and started to cry. But when he tried to clamber out, saying I'm sorry I'm sorry, she came to him then. He remembers carnation soap, her white skin's softness, hair even redder than his, how she hugged him and kissed his eyelids before he could even pretend to protest. He strokes a little faster.

Dorothea's touched. Everyone says so, even her sister Clarice, who works at the munitions factory. His aunt has tried, Lord knows she's tried, to talk Clarice into sending Dorothea out for a weekend on the farm, with his two sisters.

It's not healthy, his aunt says, spending all her time in that room with the blinds drawn. She's a big, strong girl yet. What she needs is some elbow grease to take her mind off things. And it's true, Dorothea's only a little shorter than he is, with big shoulders and strong, wide hips.

But Clarice just clams up when his aunt talks this way. Even Jimmy gets quiet when he sees Dorothea, Jimmy who makes a scabrous joke of everything now or flies into a sudden rage, hitting anything near him with his crutch. When he's around. Usually he's down at the Veteran's Hospital, though he doesn't seem to like it there. Or drinking with his buddy Ryan, who'd lost an arm at

Kasserine Pass. When Dorothea offered to cut the right leg off Big Gus's old serge pants and hem them up for him, Jimmy turned pale and hobbled out past her. That night his aunt had to bail him out of jail. He'd started a brawl at the Five Spot.

When Jimmy got home, he swung himself over to the closet in his room and started hurling all his uniforms onto his bed. Then he grabbed some scissors and cut all the ribbons and badges off them, even the First Infantry insignia he'd been so proud of, and tossed them out on the lawn. Gus crept out later and rescued them. He's got the First Infantry badge, the Big Red One, up on the flowered wall he can hear Dorothea through. She's singing:

All your fears are foolish fancy, maybe,
You know, dear, that I'm in love with you.

With the lingering clarity of a seizure, Gus imagines her in her green quilted dressing gown, her head slightly cocked, so that her fine, thin ringlets trail over one eye, like Veronica Lake. That's how she looked last Sunday when he sneaked over there. His aunt doesn't like him seeing Dorothea, he ought to be with boys and girls his own age, not mooning over grown women who aren't right in the head. When they got to the end of each song, she would open the big round eyes everyone said were her best feature, one glowing green through the scrim of her red hair. One moment she'd stare, as though to memorize everything about him. Other times it was as if she hardly saw him, looked right through to the side table piled up with old magazines, two withered African Violets, one of Jimmy's ribbons and a broken gramophone.

They worked out the changes to "What'll I Do?" and "Blues In The Night", songs that Les Brown and His Band of Renown do on the radio. He gets her to try jazzier numbers than her usual old parlour tunes, because he wants to play alto and clarinet with his older brother. If Jimmy ever starts up his dance band again. Sometimes they really hit it, Dorothea with her firm, Jellyroll Morton touch and his clarinet starting down mellow, then up, sweet and bitchy.

It's funny, he's usually come into a tissue long before this. Maybe it's the Asmidor cigarette, the hot cubeb and hemp smoke he forced down his ricketting throat till finally the torn sac of his lungs healed, stretched. Or that he jerked off an hour ago, when his aunt finally finished with her face and her hair and reminded him again to sort the Victory Drive scrap and took her second-best purse and left. Maybe because it's so hot.

It was hot last Sunday too. Dorothea had the fans on full blast and she served him Irish whisky and coke, with some lime squeezed in, a Cuba O'Libre she called it, and made him promise not to tell. When they played he stood by the piano, swaying ever so gently, just like Artie Shaw, looking down the ebony length of the clarinet at the sheet music and her.

She really liked "What'll I Do". When Dorothea took a shine to a song she threw herself into it, repeating phrases, stretching out bars with heedless rubato, swaying and plunging on her stool. She hummed along, then belted out the lines "*What'll I do\When you're so far away\And I'm alone and blue?*" in her clear, astringent alto, pushing, then dragging, the beat. It was all he could do to keep up, watch the music and try to peek down her green robe.

She caught him looking, took a deep breath and leaned forward. Blue veins meandering over white breasts, her nipples' candent pink.

He faltered, stopped in mid-note.

She stood up quickly, shoving the stool aside, stumbling as she turned. He saw a flash of red furze, a thick, twisting scar on her belly. Then she caught him by the hair on the back of the head, staring up at him. Whisky breath, carnation soap over smoker's sweat, her salty musk.

Dorothea paused, getting her balance, then leaned over and nipped him on his snub nose, softly, but not so gently as she could have, small teeth leaving furrows on sun-pink flesh.

He glimpsed movement and saw them both in the oak framed mirror on the opposite wall, red hair burning in the shadowy, clutched space, wicking light away from dark furniture hulks, dusty sunlight sifting up from them like blazing snow.

Suddenly she caught the flesh of his cheek in a twisting pinch, pulling at him while both their eyes filled with tears. "You're just like your brother," she rasped. "Just like daddy," she called toward the stroller against the wall, glowing golden around a shadowed cave of cushions and coverlets.

She turned then, and walked silently to her own room, shutting the door.

He waited a moment, wondering what to do, then went to her door and knocked, hesitantly.

When there was no answer, he left, tiptoeing down the creaky wooden stairs, careful not to let the screen door slam.

Dorothea sings:

Every cloud must have a silver lining,
Wait until the sun shines through.
Smile my honey dear, while I kiss away each tear,
Or else I shall be melancholy too.

It's quiet now, and he strains, listening, when he hears her shift, pushing the piano stool back, the slight shuffle of her slippers as she pads across the room.

There's a slow, rhythmic squeak, something rolling back and forth on the carpet, and Dorothea coos "You're a good girl, yes you are, Mummy's good little girl."

Gus stares around the room, as if he could somehow catch whatever it is Dorothea is seeing. Pink carnations open and close, polyps in a green sea. And it's there, if he just glances at it out of the corner of his eye, in Jimmy's graduation picture. The other cadets have vanished and the focus seems a little off. Maybe that's why the white dress seems to stream out towards the edges of the picture frame, as if the light were hurrying away, to another destination. And Dorothea's smile, half-hidden by her gauzy veil, casts its own light. Towards Jimmy, his arm linked with hers, beaming down at the little blurred figure who gambols round their knees.

Hardly realizing, he's been fingering the clarinet. Now he puts it slowly to his lips, moistens the reed, gets his fingering, and starts to play, breathily at first, but with growing assurance, the horn's bell toward the wall:

Come to me my melancholy baby,
Cuddle up and don't be blue...

He stops then, straining to hear something he can't quite believe. And there it is again, a baby's gurgle and coo.

The End

Crawling to the Moon, Page 118

FALL

Because the wires are tightening, I'll run with you this time, your low, soft steps spreading gravity like salve on the earth, an enormous, fretful baby, turning away, away. Leaf piles, their heatless yellow and red fires.

I usually run impatient fast on the balls of my feet, hard. Another thing between, diluting us.

Another couple with two black Labradors, dogs veering, drunken whirligigs among stubborn gray bushes. Underground, the wires. Bright and new some places, humming and lucent with adamant blue energy.

Other places, tarnished black and snarled, but pulling just the same, ratcheting everything tight. I am watching you not-watching me, as always, your soft, in-gaze, absorbed, step, step, step.

The black dogs have cornered a squirrel, its mad stare, an acorn still cramming its jaws, tiny genital sheath, a Nibelung surprised at its machinations. The blued gunbarrel sky. Even at this slow pace, my strides harder than yours, my knee swelling hot beneath its elastic wrap,tendons drawing taut.

This scene is something else to you. We don't, can't talk about it. The dogs bark. The squirrel's desperate rush. Wires in the ground, the derelict trees, the clapped-out grass, contracting, pulling together, crushing what strays between them.

We keep on, parallel, my heavy footfalls, your gentle, stubborn pace, drifting away...

The End

Crawling to the Moon, Page 120

DRAGON DILEMMA

Ka Vorgh wondered if he'd come to the wrong place. He was in a cave smelling of sulfur, which didn't bother him much, since barbarian warriors' hygienic standards weren't overly finicky. The aroma alone would have identified it as a dragon's abode even if the dead trees outside didn't each bear an armored knight's charred skeleton like a mail-clad scarecrow.

As near as he could tell, he was in the central chamber, a lofty vault transfixed with huge stalactites and stalagmites, and at one end, a massive ridge, towering like a great waterfall frozen in stone. The brimstone smell was strongest here. If ever there was a place that should be the heart of a firedrake's lair, this was it. But it also smelled of oddly of soap and was dust-free, not to mention a distinct lack of the shattered and gnawed bones any self-respecting dragon ought to have strewn about.

Most importantly, where was the trove? Every tale he'd heard told him there should be a gigantic heap here of gold, silver, weapons and jewels, round which Gloxalla had wound his scaly bulk. The only evidence of habitation he could see by the light of his torch was what looked like shelves in a far corner of the cave. Coming closer, he saw they were indeed wooden shelves, quite well made and only half full of various objects, arranged by group. There were a few crowns and tiaras on one shelf, some necklaces on the other. The edged weapons were divided into categories, straight, Western models and curved or wavy krisses, yatighans and scimitars. Small, regular stacks of different currencies. Everything was recently dusted and neatly labeled. It was all clean, orderly and, even to a Northern barbarian's undiscerning gaze, completely second-rate at best.

Crawling to the Moon, Page 121

He scratched under his loincloth and flexed his mighty thews, a habit that filled time on those occasions when there was nothing handy to slash, smash or stab. Then he noticed his torch's light gleaming off a large, iron bound trunk in a niche he hadn't seen before. Right, he thought, maybe the dragon keeps the good stuff hidden away. We'll have a look at that.

The trunk was unlocked, save for a large hook and eye, of roughly hammered wrought iron. He prised it open as quietly as he could, feeling somewhat guilty to be spending time searching for pelf when he should be rescuing the Princess. But you never know, he rationalized, there might be a charm against dragon fire in here.

The trunk proved to be full of satins, velvets and costly-looking linens, many intricately embroidered with silk and golden threads. Even in the dim torchlight Ka Vorgh could tell some were richly dyed. There were capes, girdles, robes, furbelows, scarves and many items for which he had no names. The barbarian was no fashion expert, but he knew he'd found at least a bit of real treasure. He tied a length of raw silk scarf around his forehead, wondering if it matched his eyes.

"I suppose you're King Osgalt's latest avenger." The voice was high and cultured, but the mouth it emerged from was a black-lipped and impressively fanged slash, set in a huge head covered with dull bronze scales and dominated by bulging eyes of a strange pink, like red flames behind milky glass. The dragon regarded him from atop the curtain wall, perhaps twenty good strides straight up.

In one fluid motion Ka Vorgh drew and hurled a long knife, shouting a curse that involved improbable liaisons with musk oxen. As an impromptu reaction this was reasonably good, more impressive than fainting or trying to make a break for it, which would have involved an undignified scramble to the nearest stalagmite's cover, still a long way from the cave mouth. But even mighty Northern barbarian thews weren't really up to throwing anything straight up that far and maintaining penetration velocity, particularly when the target was armored in thick bronze scales.

Or maybe they were. It was a moot question, because the would-be stabbee turned and, with deft timing, snagged the spinning dagger at the apex of its arc with a whip-like prehensile tail. "Hmm," the dragon said, dangling the blade close to its eyes and illuminating with a small, bright flame from one nostril, "good Cimmerian ironwork, not one of your cheap Stygian knock-offs. Nice boar's head pommel and the blade's runes say very flattering things about the bearer."

This stopped Ka Vorgh, who had been unsuccessfully trying to find foot- and handholds up the curtain wall while trying to stay out of the dragon's field of fire. "In truth?" he asked. "My cousin Finbold told me it was curse to make me throw like a little girl."

"I think your cousin was a bit jealous. This is quite a potent blood-seeking spell. I don't want to read it here, you understand: Can't be too careful with words of power and such. But take it me from me, this is a nifty bit of witchery."

"But it didn't work against you, Gloxalla."

"Well it might have, you know. But everything these runes promise to do is directed against your enemies."

While they talked Ka Vorgh had, by means a quick dodge, two feints, a gigantic leap and desperate duck and roll, managed to wedge himself in a niche which, while out of the firedrake's line of sight, was rather too tight for maneuvering when your shoulders were as wide as his. By dint of all this he was perhaps two strides closer to the top of the curtain wall. "But you're a dragon," he protested. "You've abducted Princess Rowbifna, slain many good knights and true. Plundered the land and the royal treasury. Of course you're my foe!"

"You know, Ka Vorgh-"

"How do you know my name, fiend?"

"I have my sources. But as I was saying, speaking as someone who's traveled a bit and met a Cimmerian or three, I wouldn't have expected a Northern barbarian to be so sensitive to the plight of a few 'good knights and true'."

"It's professional courtesy."

"Well, that courtesy gives me hope that we may yet have a civilized, if you'll pardon the term, discussion. And as for Princess Rowbifna..."

"Yoo hoo! Mr. Vorgh! Sir Mercenary Rescuer, hello-o!" Somewhat against his better judgment, Ka Vorgh craned his neck out nervously and ducked immediately back. When no fiery blast was forthcoming, he peered again, to be rewarded with a vision of an attractive woman in her mid-twenties, wrapped in a clean linen robe, standing with one arm draped around the dragon's scaly neck. She beamed at him. "Nice thews, sport."

"Erm, thanks. I try to stay in shape."

"Listen, we have a Dragon's Hostage aerobicise group. We're all supposed to meet Wednesdays but oftentimes I'm the only one there. Someone with your physique would be a big, um, inspiration to the slackers. Prithee, do you think you could--"

"What wizardry is this? This is not Princess Rowbifna or she is ensorcelled!"

"Ensorcelled? Is that what I get called for being friendly, you thick-pated, Northern--"

"Now, now, Rowy…"

"Call off your succubus, fiend!"

"I got your succubus right here, you stinking Cimmerian ape!" With this, she pulled a curved sword from a shoulder sheath. Despite being taken aback by this unmaidenly action, Ka Vorgh couldn't help admiring, in a purely professional manner, the way the draw flowed into a vicious down-slash.

"Princess, please. Mr. Vorgh has traveled a long way and been given some very bad information. Don't you think we owe him a bit of an explanation before we skewer or broil him?"

"But Gloxy, he called me--"

"I seem to remember someone promising to draw up the contract for the Mill Cooperative's Pestilence Insurance."

"But--"

"Yesterday, I think, is when they said they'd have it done…"

"Oh, all right. But call me if you decide to slay him."

"Off you go, then…"

The Princess, or succubus or whatever she might have been, sheathed her sword and flounced off through a hole in the cavern wall, though not before casting Ka Vorgh a look equal parts menace and something much more promising.

"You mustn't mind her, you know. She has her father's temper, but many more admirable qualities."

"Leave off your honeyed words, serpent. For naught shall avail you when I, Ka Vorgh--"

What he planned to say or do is a matter of pure conjecture, as this philippic was interrupted by a sheet of flame that would have roasted him where he stood, but for the barbarian's quick reflexes. He ducked back into his hidey-hole, but his hair and loincloth required some frantic extinguishing swats and his tan skin was now raspberry red.

"Kindly do not call me a serpent, Mr. Vorgh. I've been quite patient with you so far, but you happen to have caught me just before my molting time and there are limits. I imagine that where your skin hasn't crisped off it's starting to itch very badly indeed. Now consider being covered completely in ill-fitting, heavy and fiercely itchy armored scales for several weeks and I think you'll see that my good humor is not something on which you may rely."

"You don't scare me, dragon."

"Then you're not nearly bright enough to survive this encounter." There followed a silence, broken at length by a long, sizzling sigh. "How is King Osgalt these days?"

"Pale and unwell. Worried sick about his daughter and the welfare of his subjects, no thanks to you."

Gloxalla gave a snort of laughter, punctuated by a gout of green flame. "And his chief knight, Sir Donymir, how fares he?"

"Sorrowful as his liegelord, but a bold and true knight."

"He accompanied you most of the way here, did he not?"

"How did you know that, dragon?"

"All in good time. Did you ever wonder, Mr. Vorgh, why such a brave and doughty knight as Donymir hasn't rode up here, challenged me and added his name to the lists of glory?"

"He said he was bound by an evil geas."

Another fiery snort. "I'll make you a bargain, Cimmerian. Allow me to tell you a story, and if you haven't changed your mind about your mission by the end, why, I'll let you climb up here to within a sword's length of me.

Ka Vorgh considered his alternatives. His preferred option, a surprise attack, was long gone. He had a lot of climbing to do, much of it exposed and within the dragon's range, to go either up or down. If Gloxalla were true to his word, there was at least a possibility of a quick death that might merit a glorious verse of some minstrel's lay.

"Say on, firedrake. But make it not overlong. I itch for battle."

"Ka Vorgh, methinks you just itch, period. But fear not, my tale's short.

"Ahem. Once there was a king who'd just manage to gain control of a small kingdom, which he hoped to make considerably larger. He'd come to the throne in the usual way when succession was disputed, by ambush, poisoning, sneak attacks, suborned alliances and forced marriage. He hoped to turn his little nation into a great empire in the same manner.

"But now he faced a liquidity crisis. Transforming himself from one of many ambitious princelings into the king had been an expensive process, what with all the bribery, payouts for assassins, informants, mercenaries and the like. He'd used up all his ready cash and killed off many of the nobles who were strong and wealthy enough to raise more in a hurry. And the usual moneylenders had all fled because he'd been rather a difficult client and was now a bad security risk, because the neighboring kingdoms had gotten wind of his plans and resolved to attack while he was relatively weak."

"The war on the Servungian marshes, I remember that," Ka Vorgh said. "Hard fighting, mud, flies and no good plunder."

"No clear victor, more to the point. A long, dreary, costly war and there was our king with mercenary chiefs to pay, among whom was your cousin. Whatever became of Finbold, by the bye?

"I smote him with a battle-hammer."

"Quite right, too. He was a nasty piece of work. But I digress. So what did the king do? He needed backing quickly and wasn't particular about the source. So he invited, I say again, invited a dragon of the East into his kingdom, with promises of a safe haven from unruly knights and their challenges, a nice lair in some very scenic mountains, a fat bullock or two a year to munch on, and all in exchange for the dragon's extensive hoard, which treasure he pledged to repay and increase from the expected profits of his empire-building. And for a bond, the king suggested and delivered his first-born daughter as a hostage."

"A dastardly lie. Osgalt would never pawn his own kin--"

"Consider the logistics, Mr. Vorgh. As a professional, try to construct a feasible plan whereby I, a creature far more suited to crisping a regiment or two than anything so stealthy and delicate as a kidnapping, could snatch a well-guarded, vigorous young woman and spirit her away without injury.

"You have your hostage ensorcelled."

"Hostages, as I believe the princess told you. From your expression I surmise that Osgalt may have omitted that small detail. Rowbifna was the only first. I have to give Osgalt some credit for judgment there, actually. Rowbifna's an ambitious girl, more than a match for her father in intellect and spirit. She wouldn't have let niceties like patrilineality and an occupied throne stand in her way, were she back at the palace."

"Lies, base lies..." But Ka Vorgh's voice held a quaver of doubt.

"My dear fellow, you'll see the truth of my assertions sooner than you think. But as I was saying, with every new, ill-considered expedition the king incurred more expenses, each one entailing another surety, sometimes title deeds to farmland the dragon didn't fancy, (It's odd, I know, but we firedrakes actually prefer dank caves inside cold, remote mountains.) or meaningless regal writs entitling the bearer to collect outrageous taxes, were he able to travel from village to village without panicking the general population. But most often it was some royal brat or other, who'd been plucked unwillingly from his usual habits of hunting, drinking and producing armigerous bastards, drugged silly and laid out here as collateral.

"But you could have said no!"

"True enough, but, hard as it may be to credit, dragons are actually very soft-hearted creatures, a weakness that occasionally interferes with our other innate proclivity as excellent money managers. Every time I saw one of these aimless, spoiled, embittered young heirs, I confess that I yearned to give them some purpose in life beyond pointless exploitation and conquest.

"To date, the results have been mixed, I admit. But Rowbifna is my shining success, if I say so myself. It was she who gave me the idea for my present enterprise, the one that has so vexed Osgalt and provoked him to send warrior after warrior against me. Tell me, Ka Vorgh, with all the King's talk about his subjects' suffering, did you actually see any country people outside the capitol?"

"Now that you mention it, Donymir seemed loath to venture near populated areas. He claimed you had spies in all the villages, working against their neighbors."

"So you never met any villagers outside the king's immediate sway?"

"There was a party of fair-goers at the ferry. Donymir didn't want me talking to them."

"I'm sure he didn't. And how did they seem to you?"

"Prosperous, now that you mention it. Well-fed and cheerful."

"And did they cheer you on in your noble mission to free them from the dragon's dread oppression?"

"No, they seemed in haste to leave us. I heard two of them laugh when they were downstream, though one woman had looked at me with eyes full of tears."

"As soon as she'd recovered from the opium her kidnappers had laid her out with and reconciled herself to her situation, Rowbifna came to me with a startling proposition. Why squander my pelf on a royal spendthrift, she said, when I could be lending smaller, but far more crucial sums to the people of the country, who (a) really needed the money; and (b) would actually pay it back.

"Our first venture was capital investment in a new loom for a weavers' guild in the west country. Then we imported some high quality barley for the farmers and millers in a village just south of here. We financed a bridge over the river Cardagh, saving travelers' time and putting an extortionate ferryman out of business. And from there on the enterprise almost grew itself.

"The King was happy with all this, at first. Prosperous people are less likely to rebel, or so he thought. But then he went to collect his usual exorbitant taxes and found the villages in question protected by a small, but well motivated and equipped force comprised of the very royal cast-offs he'd fobbed off on me, plus any number of veterans still unpaid from his many unsuccessful wars of conquest. What's more, the village headmen told him to take up the matter of monies owing with me, if he dared.

"From then on there's been a stream of misinformed fighting men sent this way, laboring under delusions of glory and royal rewards for ridding--Hold on…" and here Gloxalla inhaled deeply, then sent a narrow stream of white fire to Ka Vorgh's left and through the portal that led to the cave's mouth. There was a scream and a flaming figure in blackened armor reeled up, hurled a lance that landed closer to Ka Vorgh than the dragon, then turned and staggered noisily out.

While the barbarian gaped, Gloxalla explained. "Here's hoping that's the last of Donymir, your good knight and true, not to mention his geas. He always meant to kill you, either when you'd dispatched me and had your guard down, thus saving on rewards, or if you were persuaded by my tale. Osgalt and his henchmen, you see, know it will only take a few more armed and aware fellows like yourself before they're on their way out for good.

"More lies", Ka Vorgh said, but his heart wasn't in it.

Crawling to the Moon, Page 128

"Really, Mr. Vorgh? Loyalty is an admirable quality, but only when tempered with judgment. Now, to business: Rowbifna and I are organizing a task force to take control of the royal treasury and we could use another enterprising fellow like you. Full benefits, a good horse, your choice of arms and armor and cut of the proceeds.

"I'm going to leave you now. Rowbifna's got a fine grasp of contract writing, but she gets a little too clever with the fine print. Besides, I'm unutterably itchy, a condition with which you may empathize. I've got some ointment back there that works nicely for humans and dragons. But before you come looking, either for relief or blood, I invite you to walk outside the cave and check on your good knight and true. If he's alive I think you'll find he's now accompanied by some other fellows who won't give you much of a welcome. Do let me know your decision as soon as possible."

"Two things, dragon."

"Yes, Mr. Vorgh?"

"How big of a cut? And what are 'benefits'?"

The End

Crawling to the Moon, Page 130

THE NEW PEOPLE

Chapter One

How do you deal with the New People? No one is really sure. You can't show them anything they haven't seen. They don't have to travel to where they want to be. They just step in from out of the air, leaving you and your friends to wait outside in line.

Anything that catches their eye, they take. You'll see a hand reach out of nowhere, out of the New Place. Sometimes, if they like a gallery, a waterfall, a person, they take it with them, leaving a blue Coin. They say you can trade these Coins for treasure, even for Real Citizenship, if you know how to read the signs that glow within them. They say there is an Angel who guards the gates of the New Place, who must do your bidding if you put the Coin in front of him where he cannot see it. They say you can buy the New Place with the right Coin, once you have shared a grave with the Beast All of Hands. No one knows what these things mean and the New People aren't saying.

* * *

Pilar often wondered why all this should have happened to her and her family. She was an ordinary woman, born in Los Angeles without citgene or papers, working as a maid in Pasadena. Conchita was the only child she'd ever have, conceived before the Popcops caught up with her. Her patrons, the McDermotts, kept them from doing Conchita, but not before they'd given Pilar The Shot without a warrant.

Crawling to the Moon, Page 131

She knew the McDermotts, rich people with a Harvest concession, could easily get The Shot reversed with New drugs or a cybermedic. Sometimes they talked vaguely of getting her and Conchita permies, but it never came to anything. She never pressed these things. She had a job and she knew she was lucky. They kept renewing Pilar's temp card and someday she hoped to get a permie, but she knew lots of people wanted full status and how many got it? Between surviving on what the McDermotts paid and trying to save for Conchita's education, she had enough trouble in her life.

And yes, her girl was pretty. She knew Mr. McDermott noticed and that was another worry. Conchita had Pilar's huge dark eyes, thick black, wavy hair and her father's tall slimness and hawk-like good looks. But surely the New People had their pick of beauties.

* * *

Since the New Ones came things are the same, but not as much so. They stride out of their Doors, high up in the cold, exhausted air, trailing breezes of summers from before you were born, laughing as they amble above the queue you wait in, scattering frangipani and half-eaten dabaloos, flanked by Tri-Vids, the little silvery balls that dart through the sky like minnows, watching everything New. The New Stars will appear in their faint cars that glide like pearl mists over the traffic jam you swelter in. They will stand swaying like tall willows in the faint breeze that seems to follow them, smiling indulgently as you overcharge them at your booth in the market, paying with the blue Scratch Coin you will never want to spend.

Conchita was playing with her dolls by the abandoned overpass, at the outskirts of Santa Esperanza where her mother's hut was. School was out and she really should be helping around the big house. But she tried to stay home as much possible, because that's where she could be alone, without Mr McDermott always making her get him this or that or putting his hands on her. She was dressing Barbie in a lograv outfit when the tall woman with the fine red chains instead of hair walked out of the concrete wall, the one covered with Aztec Lords spray holos. Conchita thought the woman looked like Barbie, but also like Dimanche, except for the chains.

* * *

Since the New People came, everything has been that much thinner. The one your husband brings home for supper will smile and *murmur, dipping a glimmering sensor in the sauce made with lemons you grew and preserved yourself. You'll know, as he does this, that you won't be able to tell the meal he generates later from your own cooking. You'll meet him later, after work. Absurdly drunk on watery beer, he'll drape his long-muscled, glowing arm over your narrow shoulders, slurring strange confidences. He'll talk about parties with Hanrahan, Mikhail-7, Silver Orchid, Dimanche and other Megastars. You'll listen with the caught-breath longing that makes belief and scepticism equally impossible.*

* * *

The Woman with Red Chains scanned around her. She was naked and her golden body was covered with designs, some with stones and chips set in them. Conchita thought she looked like she was coming from somewhere with different gravity. The woman sniffed the air. She pivoted smoothly on her left hip, turning to look into the wall, the flickering of its holo-flames. Then she stared at Conchita, as if she had just noticed that part of her surroundings was alive. She flicked out her black, spiky tongue and crooked her finger.

"Want to go somewhere New, *hermanita*?" she asked. She was smiling, but shaking her head, as if to say "No."

She sounded like Dimanche, too. Conchita remembered that line from an old viro, one of Dimanche's first hits. "Let go of you," Dimanche had sung. "Be someone New."

* * *

Since the New Ones came, there is too much of everything and not enough. Dancing past, a coppery New boy will drop something small, whirling and often green, with a shape you can never describe, as you trudge home from the office. You'll wait till he and his Tri-Vids round the corner, then snatch it up, hating yourself, not noticing the trailing TriVid watching you till too late. When the little silver ball glides in front of your face, you'll find yourself looking at Silver Orchid's tiny projection. She'll ask you if you know what you have and you'll stammer and run. You'll lie awake that night and others, worrying about whether the Beast All of Hands will show up to claim it. The New People say there is no Beast All of Hands, even though your cousin says she knows someone who has a friend who saw it. Hanrahan himself went on TriVid to deny it.

"All sales are final," he said.

Conchita looked around, though she knew the woman was talking to her. She stared up at Casa Pablo Huong, the mayor's cardboard and mud compound on the top of the hill. She heard Otis, their village donkey, bray as Pablo trudged out to give him his feedbag and his short rest from pumping the barrio's water. There were shots in the distance. She heard her mother calling.

As she turned to answer, the Woman with Red Chains touched her shoulder. It tingled where the slim, golden hand rested. She looked down at her blouse. It was New, it was something she had seen in viros. It smelled like sandalwood. Slow patterns undulated through the weave. The woman lifted her hand and Conchita's blouse was what she put on that morning, most mornings, a stitchless piece of Agency acrylic, tarnished with age. She looked down at lo-grav Barbie. She was getting too old to play with dolls and anyway, Barbie wasn't New. She dropped it. She turned to the woman. "OK," she said.

The Woman with Red Chains smiled with one side of her face. "Come on then," she said, in a voice that was somehow different. Then she delicately spat a blue, glowing Coin onto the ground between them. Without thinking, Conchita stooped to pick it up. She couldn't make out the still blurry Face within it, though the Hand was clear enough. It was light and the edge thick and round, not sharp like they said the really valuable ones were. Somehow, it seemed almost soft. She was going to squeeze it when the Woman with Red Chains grasped her again. This time, Conchita's arm went numb and she dropped the Coin. Locking eyes with Conchita, the Woman ran the Coin lightly along the girl's forearm. A thin line of blood appeared, though Conchita couldn't feel any cutting. This the Woman licked with her black, spiky tongue and the blood disappeared. Not letting go, the Woman moved back in measured, formal steps, like someone doing a court dance. One, two, three and they were through the wall and someplace Else.

Chapter Two

One will gesture and the machine he carries, the one you can almost see, will give him a starry new sky, cool, with Venus in the Fourth House and a bulbul calling from the cypress tree. While the office lights buzz, he'll lean back on the cracked chair, breathing the jasmine scented breeze, waiting for you to check his passport, smiling for the Tri-Vids. On the phone, while you watch them stagger, giggling and blowing golden flutes, perpendicularly up the side of the bank towers across from your two-room apartment on the 243rd floor, Mary Ellen will say she hardly notices them. But later, reaching under the bed at her place, you'll find three Hanrahan biochips and some well-worn holos of Scimitar, Dimanche and Kris K on a little altar.

* * *

When Pilar got home and could not find her daughter, she ran around the village, calling. Finally someone told her that Octavio, leader of the Aztec Lords, had the blue Coin the New People leave when they take something. No one wanted to go, but when she began to cry, Pablo Huong said he would come with her to see the Lords.

* * *

Waiting, you don't know for what, you'll watch the New Person on your shift at the factory, the sad one, who doesn't seem to talk to the others. And when he doesn't show up for work one day or ever again, you'll doubt the foreman's explanation. But at the same time you'll shake your head and shrug, because you knew, you always knew he wouldn't stay. And you'll look, furtively, like everyone else does, to see if he left a Scratch Coin somewhere among the machines.

* * *

They came to a big house on a hill. It was made in the shape of a skeletal coiled rattlesnake, the Bone Fortress, stronghold of the Aztec

Lords. You could see right through the spaces between the white ribs to the sky beyond, but Pablo knew that was because New optic field generators bent light away from the gang's living quarters, storerooms and armories. In front of the head sat two gangboys fitted into smartgun harnesses. They were smoking and watching a tri-vid of the tele-merc who'd won this year's Deathmatch and became New, but their smartguns shifted and covered Pilar and Pablo as soon as they started climbing the hill.

One of them, tall and skinny with a red plastic eye that didn't fit well, sauntered over to check them out. "*Hola*," he said, sounding bored. "State your business."

"I want to see Octavio," Pilar said, looking him in his human eye and holding up a gringo silver dollar. He didn't seem surprised. How many mothers, Pilar wondered, came here every week looking for their children?

He sneered at the old coin, but he took it. He frisked them thoroughly, lingering on Pilar's breasts and hips, then shook his head at the other, looking a little disappointed. The other, a squat man whose face had a moving tattoo of a spider killing and wrapping a moth, walked over to the head, where he rapidly fingerprint identified himself and punched in a digital code on a touchpad hanging under one of the nostrils. He did this all without taking his eyes off the tri-vid screen.

While they waited for a response, Red Plastic Eye fished a couple of black cloth bags out of a cardboard box by the snake's jaw. He tossed them to Pablo and Pilar and motioned them to put them on. Pilar fumbled hers and was just picking it up when the snake's jaws opened slowly with a deep hiss and the tail rattled behind her. In the shadow between the fangs she saw a pair of legs shod in New, expensive bootsneaks, the kind Scimitar sang about. Red Plastic Eye followed her glance. He frowned, but contented himself with taking the hood from her, roughly shoving it down on her head and tying the drawstring at the bottom tighter than he needed to. Then he pushed them, first Pablo, then her, into the snake's mouth, ducking them like a cop shoving a perp into the back of a squad car. For people like them los Senores didn't bother with the full, fangs-out gape. Even short Pilar had to bend low to get in.

Inside, air in the snake's mouth smelled of sweat, gun oil and astringent chemicals. The gangbanger waiting for them said "Aqui,

aqui," impatiently, like a man late for an appointment. When they had crawled close enough he pulled them upright and led them brusquely down a curving hall and through several doors. Like the others, his discipline seemed lax. He didn't handcuff them, check their hoods, spin them around, make any switchbacks or try to confuse them. At length he shoved them stumbling into what Pilar could tell was a large open space.

Pablo and Pilar stood there uncertainly, afraid to move. The inside of Pilar's hood stank of another's fearful sweat and rank breath. They could hear their escort's footfalls going back the way they came and rough, slurred voices conversing in front of them. Someone said "*Mierda*, where did you get those nines?"

Someone else said "Don't just stand there, you stupid chingas. Take those things off and let's have a look at you."

They pulled their hoods off and Pilar saw they were standing in a dusty courtyard, in front of an old clawfooted mahogany table, its surface raddled with carved initials, cigarette burns and spray-holos. Three gangbangers sat there woozily in the midday sun, playing something involving cards and knives jammed into the tabletop. One leered and waggled his tongue at her. Another backhanded him as if he'd done this many times before and nodded as if Pilar and the mayor were expected. He motioned her toward a lounge chair in at the back. Octavio was lying there under a big sun umbrella, the only shade in the courtyard, flipping a sapphire Coin back and forth on his new abdominal muscles. Seeing it, Pilar would have rushed screaming at the Warlord, if Pablo hadn't grabbed her shoulder. She almost shook him off before she saw what he was pointing at. A slim but muscular man with jaguar hair danced silently around the compound, face hidden by his virovisor, hands and feet a whir of holoed blades, whips and guns.

"*Buenas dias, Jefe*," said Pablo Huong, when Octavio nodded to them. The silent dancer spun around them, hands and arms bristling with wires and sensors. Then he somersaulted over their heads, landing, flexed and light, near the card players. They never glanced at him, but somehow the cards came down more crisply and hands hovered by knives.

"*Hola*, Lord Mayor, *Mamacita*. Hector!" Octavio snapped his long, steel fingers. The holo-player stopped, de-opaqued the visor, produced three glasses of yage tequila from somewhere, served them

Crawling to the Moon, Page 137

and went back to his viro, the latest BodyKnife BattleWorld. Pilar would not, could not drink, for fear she would start shouting if she opened her mouth, so Pablo Huong downed hers before he spoke.

"Jefe, this woman's daughter may be missing."

"A daughter, eh?" said Octavio, examining the blue Coin's still-forming Face with his gunsight eye. "How old?"

"Twelve."

"Hector, have we taken in any twelve year old girls lately?"

Hector corkscrewed in mid-air, slashing invisible foes while he thought. "How lately?"

"Today. Two hours ago," said Pablo.

"Not today, no."

Octavio shrugged at his guests. "I guess you will have keep looking."

Pablo Huong was about to concede this before Pilar caught his eye. "Actually, Jefe," he said, "we know... that is... we believe... that the Aztec Lords may have some interest in this matter..."

"What has this to do with us?"

"She thinks the New People may have taken her. She believes that they may have left one of their Coins."

"A Coin? Something like this Scratch here?"

"Something like it, yes."

"Let us say that something like this is true and that this is that token. What would she like me to do about this matter?"

"Find her!" shouted Pilar.

"Oye, Mamacita, look around you. Do we look like skip tracers?"

"Big man," she sneered, "are you afraid of the Angels?"

"Hector! *Mamacita* says we're scared of the Angels!"

Hector leaped at the willow tree, spinning upwards around the trunk to hang by one leg in a defensive stance. He frowned, slightly, running a hand through his gold and black rosetted hair. "The Angels can be dealt with, if you can reach them." His hands and free leg whistled and blurred as they jabbed and cut in glittering arabesques.

"There's your problem," said Octavio, turning back to Pablo Huong. "If you can reach them. Not to mention," flipping the coin and nodding at Pilar, "the price."

"I work for the McDermotts, who have a Harvest concession. Help me find Conchita and I will bring you through their Gate, where you can take what you want from the New Place."

Octavio grinned and Pilar knew he'd known this all along. "Now this, at least, is a proposition. Hector!"

* * *

This is what a real Coin is like: Blue, blue like they say the sky used to be, blue to freeze your eyes, blue like the glow at the edge of a black hole, where space says goodbye. On one side is The Hand That Takes and Gives. Some say it's Hanrahan's hand. Somehow you know it's big and grips with a glacier's weight. On the other side is The Face. You know it when you see it, but sometimes it's old, sometimes young, sometimes male, sometimes a woman. Some Coins are said to bear a Beast, a scavenger with long, jagged claws and huge, bonecrushing teeth. These are the old ones, thin and sharp, the ones that can buy everything and then some. Some old people say they can scratch between, though no one knows what that means.

* * *

Conchita and the Woman with Red Chains stepped through to the New Place, in a valley of tall trees and drifting opal mists. The Beast All of Hands was there, behind a rock, waiting for them. It rolled out hissing, a metre-high ball of hands with fingers sprouting hands with fingers sprouting hands, all rubbing and clutching. Conchita screamed. Somewhere beneath she saw flashes of a lamprey mouth lined with rows of needle teeth. The Woman with Red Chains stepped in front of her. She reached out and there was a spark. The Beast stopped. "Walk backwards," she said. "He smells the Coin on you."

Conchita did as she said and finally the Beast All of Hands rolled off into the mists, its million fingers scrabbling at the earth, grabbing grass and rocks, pulling it along, like a malevolent moving coral.

"I've changed my mind," said Conchita. "I want to go back to my village." In answer, the woman reached for a gnarled trunk. It writhed at her touch and Conchita saw it was a huge, gray-green serpent, whipping its coils free. Hissing, it darted at her.

But when the great mouth gaped, it was full of fruit, yellow, red, blue and colours without name. The woman reached in and picked a purple-green curly thing. She smiled, broke it open and handed half to Conchita, still frozen in shock. It was full of custardy, lilac-scented pulp.

Conchita had only had some coca-pulque and a piece of soyjerk since she woke up, but she didn't bite until the woman pushed the fruit toward her mouth. As soon as she swallowed, the vision began.

* * *

We knew a family in the next valley who bragged that their land was owned by the New People. The mother wore a blue coin in a necklace, surrounded by shell beads. We thought they were putting on airs with a fake Coin: What would the New Ones want with rough villagers like that? Then one day in the market place I saw the mother and her two youngest children. They had all the things they owned piled around them, the wooden chests they sat on, a rug she had woven, some chickens in a cage. I didn't see the father or the older sons anywhere. The children were asking passers-by for money or food. The little boy saw me and started to say hello, but his mother pulled him away. She wasn't wearing her necklace. I walked away without looking back. I never told my parents what I saw.

* * *

In Conchita's vision, she was grown up. She couldn't tell how much older she was, because she was New and beautiful, with long raven hair and bronze skin, set with jewels. She rode in a parade through her village in a car that was also a dress and a cloud, but at the same time she was in the New Place, dancing through galactic clouds with Mikhail-7, Noelle Ling, Hanrahan and Catamount, the cheers and tinny music of her village coming to her like a distant breeze over the orchestra of the New Place.

Then a call, like a bird and like a cough, echoed through the valley. In Conchita's vision the stars dimmed and the music faded. She chewed more of the fruit, but it didn't help. The serpent turned to tree trunk again and the mists were thicker and grayer. The Woman with Red Chains turned, motioning Conchita to follow, down a path that glowed under her feet and faded as she passed.

Conchita felt groggy, like a sleeper waking from a long dream. "Wait" she said weakly, but the woman took no notice, rapidly fading into the darkening mists. Finally, just before her guide disappeared completely, the girl's nerve broke. "Wait. Wait for me," she called again, running clumsily behind.

The woman smiled over her shoulder as she caught up, but said nothing and kept striding down the steep, glowing path.

In a little while they came to a sudden canyon, a crooked knife-gouge at their feet. Miles down was a slash of a river, hurtling over fisted rocks and shooting a thousand colours in the cold, white sun. From so far away it seemed not to roar but to clatter and scream. Conchita paused to catch her breath, watching her guide, who seemed to be waiting to answer her questions.

But before Conchita could speak, the woman stepped deliberately into the void, tumbling headlong into the chasm. Too stunned even to scream, the girl watched the golden body pitch down end over end, the red chains flailing out like a tiny, crazy flower.

Chapter Three

Where the New People come from is not anywhere you can go. After the honeymoon, your daughter will call. "How are you?" you'll ask. She's fine, really, just fine. "Where are you calling from?" Well, that's difficult to say. It's close, really. "How's everything?" It's wonderful, it's... different. It's just... different. You'll see her in a couple of days and you'll realize that she's right. It's all different.

* * *

As they waited in one of the Aztec Lords' chopped-down, armoured, stretch Hyundais, Pilar studied Hector while he played one of his viros. He was probably young, she thought, but so covered with scars it was hard to tell. Some were patterned, ornamental, tattooed silver. Others jagged, random. They were in the afternoon traffic jam, La Congestíon, on the way to Pasadena, where the McDermotts lived and kept their Gate. They watched a New Person, a mile-long Chinese dragon, pass through the soot-coloured sky overhead. Hector had turned off the unlicensed manual override and settled back in his seat.

"Why do you follow him?" she asked.

He paused, and she sensed him closing down screen windows behind his eyes. "Octavio? He is el Jefe."

"But why is that? He's small. They say he's greedy, and demands more than his share. That he has to get liposuction, new blood and muscles every year, because he won't move or stop gorging himself. You're fast and strong. Why do you obey him?"

"He has *mi Animo*."

"All of us have self-will."

"I don't. Octavio took that, long ago." And he showed her the fine, silver threads that circled both his wrists, then wound around his arms and neck, to where they ran into his head through the middle of tiny red orchids, tattooed behind both ears.

"What would happen if you were to cut your threads?"

"Big Luis of Los Demonios cut his three months ago. Then he killed 15 people with his teeth and nails and died, screaming, blood shooting through the pores in his skin."

"But how will you go through the Gate, if Octavio holds your Animo? He can't reach you in the New Place."

"That's true. For this thing, Octavio has lent me back my will, temporarily."

"And what will you do, if we come back from the New Place? When your Jefe puts you back under his thumb?"

Hector didn't answer.

* * *

There are those who try to rob and murder the New People. But how do you mug a woman whose body turns to a mass of needle crystals when you reach to grab her? Or shoot a man continually dissolving to and coalescing from clove smoke and musk? If some miracle put Hanrahan within your grasp, would you pull your knife or fall down on your knees?

Conchita stood dumbly at the edge of the gorge, staring at the spot where the Woman with Red Chains had vanished in the flashing, clattering river. She didn't know what to do.

Then she noticed that the river was changing, somehow. It seemed to be swelling. No--it was rising, leaving its banks and floating upwards, faster and faster. Then the flood parted and she saw the golden figure, standing whole and apparently unhurt amid the waters.

But they weren't waters. As they drew nearer and nearer, she could see they were shards of--it looked like--it was--pottery and glass. Shattered white porcelain, splinters of green canning jars, flinders of rose-patterned boneware, bits of stained church windows, earthenware scraps and broken beer steins, they all hurtled on, scraping, squeaking and banging, except where the Woman with Red Chains stood, on a tiny island of still, flat-stacked shards.

The river rose to the edge of the gorge. The woman turned and began walking across to the cliff on the other side. Wherever she stepped, the fragments stopped and waited, edges flat, for her to pass.

Crawling to the Moon, Page 144

She smiled her strange smile over her left shoulder, motioning Conchita to follow.

"No!" she said. The woman kept walking. "Take me back! I'm afraid of heights!" The woman had reached the other cliff and was climbing it. "The splinters--they'll cut my feet!" She was almost out of sight. "Stop! I'll--Wait!" Closing her eyes, Conchita stepped into the chasm.

Below her feet she could feel the shards slow and stop, vibrating like an enormous engine. She didn't look down. Sometimes she sank in the flood and she could see glittering slivers flashing razor edges up above her head, hissing and racketing. But she closed her eyes and kept walking. And nothing cut or even scraped her.

Finally, she reached the gray cliff at the other side. And there was the Woman with Red Chains, smiling down from its summit, a few feet above her. "I'm glad you crossed quickly," she said in a low voice. "I couldn't have held the Broken River much longer."

Conchita turned just in time to see the shards topple, a flock of glittering birds, diving down into the gorge.

* * *

"Hello, Pilar," said the McDermotts' door. "We weren't expecting you just yet. Have you left something here?"

"I left something in my locker. Will you let me in, *por favor?*" Pilar usually said "please", but she had learned that the McDermotts liked her to lard her speech with a few Spanish words.

"I have monitored your locker, Pilar. There seems to be nothing that we have not issued you in there."

"Could you check the contents of my first aid kit? I put some remedies in there for Conchita's allergies."

"There are six non-standard capsules in one of the vials. I'm afraid that this is a violation of our protocol, Pilar. We're going to have to dock some of your wage points. I do hope none of them are controlled substances, dear."

"No, no, just medicine from my herb doctor. Could you let me in, please?"

"Very well, but be sure to leave one in the analyser before you leave."

"*Claro.*"

"Commencing Entrance Key sequence. . . I'm getting an anomalous reading from—— That was all the door had time to say before Hector came out of his mirrored TangleWrap and jimmied the Key. Tiny blue sparks played along the silver threads in his arms and his eyes went blank and dull as the wires extruded themselves from his palms. Then the door clicked open. He blinked and they stepped in, onto the Chinese silk rug in the foyer.

Inside, it was just the same. Mr. McDermott was snoozing on the patio lounge field, a tall gin and tonic (make sure the lime slice is fresh) half-finished by his side. He had left his flexercise bracelets on, which always made him unbearably itchy. Pilar almost started taking them off before she looked at Hector and stopped herself. She strode past, but stopped when she realized Hector was still standing there, staring at the lightly snoring, naked, recumbent man floating three feet off the floor.

"Why isn't there an alarm to wake him up?"

"The house's subsystems deal with security problems. He'll be sedated till the all-clear."

"Why don't we take him with us and make him open the Gate?"

"That wouldn't work."

"But I could kill him."

"It's all archived."

Hector rapidly scanned the room, wires glowing, and Pilar watched his eyes change as he monitored different frequencies. "I can't find any recording equipment," he said.

"Oh, it's here," she assured him. "They have a Zone Blue feed, remember. Anything you can strap yourself with, you have to buy from the New People, after they've worked out the counters. Mr. McDermott told me how it worked."

"But I could still kill him."

"I told you: It's archived. There's a Matrix in the New Place, with their somatypes, sensory map settings, long and short term mnemo-gestalts. It's updated every week. Tuesdays."

"He told you this?"

"Si."

"He could have been lying."

"He could have. Do you want to find out now, or do you want to go to the Gate?"

"*Mierda.* Let's go."

They passed through the gym, where Mrs. (Call me Emily) McDermott was in a SensDep field, working on her opera Saint Di, bodsynthing herself into all of the roles. Pilar knew she was just putting the final touches on the scene where the poor orphan Di is visited by the Angel Elton, who tells her to seek the Sacred Vaccine in Calcutta, just before she meets the future King Jayeffkay. Call me Emily had left a v-note on the black side of her SensDep, reminding Pilar to make sure she had a suite of LiveGowns ready for tomorrow's dinner party. The note chattered at her as they went by.

Pilar motioned Hector toward the back of the house, where the emergency stairs were. She couldn't remember if anyone had ever walked on them and wasn't sure they would bear their weight, but she was afraid to use the UpField for fear of countermeasures. While he checked them for traps, a long-disused projector configured itself and beamed in a holo of Mr. and Mrs. McDermott, done about two years ago, to judge from the somamodes. Their mouths moved soundlessly at first, because the Aztec Lord had ripped out the SmartFils.

The filaments grew back and reconnected as Pilar and Hector started up the stairs. Mrs. McDermott said "--concerned about your future, Gabriella—

"Which, frankly speaking, is going to be very short, if you don't give yourself up right now, you little *puta*," said Mr. McDermott.

"Why does she call you Gabriella?" asked Hector, running his hands over the risers above them.

"That was the last maid. They didn't bother to update."

"What happened to her?"

"You don't ask these things."

"Intruders," said Mr. McDermott, "you have failed to respond to repeated warnings." There was a hiss and clicking within the walls. "Failure to turn back and surrender immediately will mean that in 60 seconds this area will be an unlimited phage zone. All residual biota will be maserstructed. Countdown begins now: 60, 59, 58—

"Chinga! I don't have any good nano-stops!" Hector said.

"He doesn't have any phages."

"No?"

"Before I got here, they didn't format the House very well and they couldn't get it to follow the bio instalment schedule, so their security phages kept devolving and getting masered down. Finally, one mutated into a Breaker and escaped. It started getting multiplying and getting nasty, picking up e. coli genes and stinking the place up. They had to quarantine the House and really zap everything. They've never got around to re-installing."

"How do you know this?"

"LaVonda, the maintenance lady, told me. All we have to do is get to the Gate. They won't use any radiation or projectiles around there. The New People don't like it."

"Where is it?"

"Through those doors."

Pilar waited in front of the gray metal double doors while Hector checked them, his hands and arms bristling with probing wires and small sampling devices. He moved slowly around the periphery, then from top to bottom, doubling back often and re-checking on different wave lengths. Finally she said, "Hurry--the backup security will be coming soon."

"People or New People?"

"I don't know--I've never seen them. People, I think--the New People don't like to be bothered."

"OK, I think it's clear," Hector said, pushing her to one side and cautiously pulling open a door.

Inside was a long, bare, gray room with a high ceiling. There was a Transfer Field at the other end. Hector had never seen one before, except the momentary flash when New People or their Artifacts came through. Though he knew better, he found his gaze drawn toward the ceaseless patterns, their ghost colours snaking through the square, blank hole in the air. Mouth slack, he edged toward it, till Pilar raked her nails across his cheek. He turned to her, too dazed even to raise his hand.

"Not like that," she said. "You can't go to the New Place like that. You will fall and fall through the Place That Is Not a Place."

"How do you know? It leads to the New Place, doesn't it? What difference does it make how you go through?"

"Someone told me."

"Who?"

"Gabriella."

"When did she--"

"It doesn't matter. The backup security will be here soon."

"OK, but how do we go through, then?"

"Keep your eyes down. Think about where you are going, but not too much. Be still. Be ready."

"You're right. I have forgotten my discipline. I--"

The sirens went off then, needlers and subsonics. Hector's vision blurred and his bowels went slack as Pilar shoved him through the Gate.

Crawling to the Moon, Page 150

Chapter Four

Conchita and the Woman with Red Chains came to a squat dun building, surrounded by big, slumpy trees and an overgrown thorn hedge, steaming bitter red smoke. All the way through fields of maroon grass whispering to scribbly butterflies, the girl questioned her guide. But the woman had fallen silent again and only smiled as little cobalt flowers bloomed wherever she stepped.

As the woman forced the huge wrought iron gate open against the thorny bushes choking it in branches and fumes, Conchita heard the strange sound again, half birdcall, half cough. And as they walked up the rutted, grassed over drive, dodging growling ochre mushrooms shuffling slowly toward them, puffing noxious dust, she heard other sounds, low bubblings and squeakings and old voices muttering on and on and on...

The door was wide, heavy, deeply carved in figures that looked like oblong, heavy birds. Dirty, faded green paint flaked off dark wood. It had neither handle nor bell nor knocker. The Woman with Red Chains did something with more fingers than Conchita had seen on her hands before and it slid away, squeaking a little. From the shadows, a smell hit them: Urine, disinfectant, sweat, medicine and old cooking. There was a thin howl from somewhere.

Conchita didn't want to go in. She edged away, looking back toward the gate. But the Woman with Red Chains grabbed her, long, many fingers snaking around her arm. First it hurt where she touched, then burned, then Conchita had a feeling she couldn't understand and finally she knew she would have to enter Edge House, which was what the building was called.

As she walked slowly into the darkness, the woman at her back, Conchita put an exploratory hand out...

And touched a thing like an icy cobweb around hard vacuum. Her arm was wrenched in, up to the elbow, before she could pull back. A clattering yelp--a blue flash. She thought she saw a shape like one of the door carvings jumping back to a place that wasn't there before, but she couldn't be sure. She gulped hard against a spurt of vomit. Her hand felt numb.

Then the Woman with Red Chains pushed her and she stumbled through an old-fashioned bead curtain. Inside it was like sunlight at the end of a long August desert afternoon, with a cool wind coming from the east, except when someone coughed and she could see the long rows of beds and the machines with their dials, counters and tubing, in the thin, trembling light.

Someone was calling her.

* * *

There are those who say that there are no New People, no New Place in which they pitch their pearly tents, their flowering castles. The Skeptics see the hands that come out of purple clouds, hands that steal our fruits in the market. They see the boys who swim like dolphins through air and mountains, the women whose bodies are feathers and clockwork. They see these things and call them the Lies of Unattainable Vision, the Monetary Mirage. But they can't explain the Scratch, the way the Coins glow and cut.

* * *

They lay face down where they'd fallen on the floor. Pilar had been lucky; she'd fallen on top of Hector, cushioning her landing. Hector had managed to get one arm up, but had bruised his nose on the blue flagstones. It was hard to tell how long they were there before anyone came in. But after a time Pilar heard clicking footsteps passing by her head, quick and high at first, like mice wearing hard-soled shoes. Abruptly the sound shifted lower and within herself she felt her heart quicken, from a glacial grinding to its normal pace.

A voice came to her, inside her head. She didn't know the words, but she knew it meant "Get up".

The footsteps went on, moving about her. Then she could feel her body, blood running through her limbs. It hurt. Below her, Hector was beginning to stir. She rolled off him, raised her head, got her legs beneath her and stood, slowly, dizzily. Her head ached. Everything was too bright.

They were in a huge room, among piles of things, some in boxes or vats or refrigeration units, some lying out loose. There were heaps of flowers, other people and animals in containment fields. There

Crawling to the Moon, Page 152

were wine barrels and big rounds of cheese. There were trees and a little meadow, going brown around the edges. In a tank of faintly pink liquid, there were bristly black shrimp-things guarding a giant gold and green fruit.

Every so often, Pilar would catch a glimpse of someone moving and an area of goods would disappear, leaving bare blue slate. While she watched and waited, Hector got to his feet. He didn't say anything to her, just settled himself into a ready stance, hands up, eyes moving but empty.

At last they were the only things left in the middle of the vast, bare floor. The Angel came for them then.

At first it was hard to look at it. Depending on the angle of her gaze, Pilar saw either a faint glimmer or a blinding dazzle. She shook her head, closing her eyes. The rush of voices in her skull, all shouting different languages, made her wince and cover her ears, though this didn't help.

Then it was quiet and a single, calm voice began to count to three, over and over again, each time in a different language or dialect. When it said these words in the Angeleno patois Pilar had spoken since she was girl, the voice stopped.

The Angel coalesced before her then, as a huge, broad-chested man, seated behind a massive carved mahogany planter's desk on a marble dais, his big, clean hands folded in front of him. He wore a snowy guyabera shirt, a cream straw Stetson and high, dark boots. His heavy, pale face was ageless, black hair thick and glossy, dark eyes assessing her as one studies a brood mare. He seemed like what Pilar had often her imagined her father to be. But in a corner of her mind she knew he resembled an actor in an old Mexican soap opera she had watched as a little girl folding rich people's clothes in front of their old tri-vid, while her mother ironed and cooked.

"Why are you here?" His dark voice shook the floor beneath her feet. The harsh light behind him pinned her like a bug in a collection.

"Por favor--", Pilar began, then stopped. She was suddenly afraid to say why she had come to this place.

"Mujer," the voice pounded in her bones, "we demand to know why you and the soulless gang vermin with you have stolen into this holy realm, still smelling of the shithole that is your only home, to foul our world with your touch, to spread contagion with your every breath, to profane it with looking upon things forbidden you and yours forever. Tell me now and I will make your death quick."

Pilar began to weep. She wanted to run to somewhere low and dim. But digging in her purse for a handkerchief, she saw it there, among the lottery tickets, pills, good luck charms and wadded tissues, a blue gleam. She held the token up in front of her, flashing in the hard, white light.

The Angel sighed, a tired, disgusted sound. He shook his head and Pilar saw the faint circular depression in the middle of his wide brow. "Another beggar with a bit of glass," he muttered. The light behind him softened a little and his voice faded to a rumble. "Not one of you seems to realize that your whole miserable world runs on almost nothing but counterfeit tokens," he said, his tone almost kind. "We'd wipe out all the Earther glassworks, but you'd only pester us with plastic poker chips. In fact," he eyed the blue disc Pilar gripped, "that's exactly what it looks like." He sighed. "Best end this quickly, then. Bring it up here. At least I can have a laugh."

Slowly, her body stiff and heavy, eyes downcast, Pilar advanced to the Angel's desk. Hector kept pace, shuffling like an old man whose legs were dying slightly faster than the rest of him. The Angel ignored them, writing something in a little golden palmtop.

But when Pilar had climbed the three marble steps and began to lower the token to the glowing dark wood of his desk, his scowl stopped her. "Did I say I wanted the trash set before me, *mujer?* Hold it out, that's all."

He glanced at it, then stopped. A slow grin spread over his face and he started to chuckle low, building to a basso roar. "Oh, this is good!" he said. "Never in all my time here have I seen so obvious a fake. You must have looked long and hard for something so cheap."

"But I--my daughter--you must--"

"You forget yourself, woman. No groundscum tells a Real Citizen what he must do. No, I told you before, do not set that trash before me!" Before she could put the token on his desk, he slapped her hand, sending the blue coin flying onto the floor.

Pilar screamed and dived for the token. But before she could reach it, a weight landed on her back, knocking the wind out of her. Sprawled across her, Hector grabbed the sapphire disc. With a strength she'd never felt before, Pilar drew his hand down and bit it. The Angel's huge laughter caromed around them as they grappled.

Hector hit her with his free hand. He got his bitten hand free, still holding the token, as Pilar gathered herself to strike again.

Suddenly, Hector was off her, pivoting, his whole body an arcing stroke, arm a blue-flashing whipcrack. The Angel's guffaws were choked into a high, strange scream.

Hector pulled Pilar to her feet. "Quickly!" He hauled her up the steps of the dais, then vaulted over the big desk and onto the Angel, who had fallen out of his big leather chair, writhing on the blue-veined white marble. The Angel's eyes were glazed, askew. His big hands spasmodically groped for the blue coin, halfway embedded in the side of his neck.

Hector grabbed the thick wrists. "Get the coin to his forehead," he yelled, as the Angel growled and tried to throw him off. Though the big man writhed and lashed his head about, Pilar managed to grip the blue token. Already it felt thinner, sharper. There was no bleeding, just a cold sponginess where the disk had sunk halfway in. It came out easily, dripping a thin, yellowish ichor. The Angel began to thrash with redoubled strength, thick body arched, nearly throwing Hector off. "Hurry," he panted, the two huge paws almost at his throat.

Pilar grabbed the windmilling head and was pulled off balance, bruising her shoulder on the slate floor. The Angel bit her through her blouse. His hands were around Hector's neck when she slapped the token into the round shallow depression in his forehead. He stiffened, then collapsed with a moan that clattered, as if he were full of loose parts.

Hector rolled away, panting. "He's yours," he said.

The Angel opened his eyes, now a flat gray. "You cannot hold me like this," he whined. "Let me go, and we will forget your trespass."

Pilar got to her feet, staring down at him. "Stand up," she said. The Angel staggered to his feet as if yanked by invisible strings. His skin was dull and didn't seem to fit well. "Now take me to my daughter," Pilar ordered. The Angel turned.

"No, stop," she said. "What is your name?"

"I don't have a name, *mujer*," he said in a voice like a rusty hinge.

"Don't lie to me! Give me your name."

"The one who rides us took my name from me. He never gave me a new one."

Pilar glanced at Hector, who shrugged. "Very well," she said. "Listen to me, thing. Someone like you, from this place, took my little girl from me, my Conchita, the only child I'll ever have. Do you understand?"

"Yes."

"Now you must do as I tell you, is that right?"

The Angel nodded.

"No! I want to hear you say it!"

The Angel said "I must do as you say", as if each word were a burden he shouldered.

"I want you to tear yourself to pieces. Gouge your eyes out. Rip your belly open. Gash your throat – Stop!" she yelled, as the Angel's taloned fingers reached for his face. He stood, trembling. "Now answer me. Do you know where Conchita is?"

"No."

"Do you know how to find her?"

"Yes."

"Thing, if you run away or lead us into a trap or take one step that does not go toward Conchita, I tell you now that you must do as I have said, claw and rip and gouge and yank yourself to pieces, your hands still scrabbling long after your eyes lie blind on the ground, long after your mouth has shrieked its last. Do you understand?"

"Yes."

"Now take me to my daughter."

Silently, the Angel turned. He gestured and a door opened in the wall behind him. He stepped through and they followed.

Chapter Five

Don't think too hard about the New People, the New Place, the deal Hanrahan made or what it means for you. Ignore the beggar woman with a cracked piece of blue glass glued to her scabby forehead, howling prophesy as you pass her on the way to your job at the stock exchange, where your boss is worried about a rumour that Dimanche or some other New Icon has signed with a rival LifeLine. Take your pay home and when your son wants half of it for Scimitar implants, don't let it get to you.

* * *

Conchita walked toward the voice, down the centre of the long room filled with beds. Some were empty, but most had occupants, men, women, giants, sprites, an ape or two, a merman like an old New Icon whose name she couldn't remember, many creatures she couldn't name and some she couldn't describe. Some beds had their own atmosphere, some their own gravity. There were monitors, gro-membranes, IV drips, pumps, glass wombs, tachyon assemblers, iron lungs, electrodes, glion regenerators, webs of tubing, cable and dimensional bypass threads, all of them hooked to bodies, naked, scaly, fur-covered, in gray pyjamas, buried under sheets, a-twitch with wires, floating in gray oil.

As her bare feet padded down the concrete floor, Conchita felt a wave of eyes tracking her, following until the next row saw her, again and again. A muttering shadowed her, growing as she neared the dim end of the hall, where a voice wheezed her name. She walked by a bed under a tumorous cloud, raining, raining, and a dark vine-thing grabbed at her. She screamed, then huddled, whimpering, while the Woman with Red Chains tore off tendrils that hooted and spat. She could hardly keep from scratching herself bloody where it had touched her.

She came to a dim corner where dull pink walls smelled of piss and old cooking. Tubes and cords hung thick as jungle lianas here, festooned with yellowed paper snowflakes, glass ornaments whose faded colours barely showed through dust, twined over and again with winking strings of lights, biolumes over fibops over ancient electric bulbs. A hand fumbled out from under the sheet. A cough-raw voice breathed her name. Conchita heard a creak and a rustle behind her. She turned to see the Woman with Red Chains down the hall, shoving her way into a bed, hampered by something heavy under the covers. At last she drew both legs up and kicked, sending the body flopping, thudding into the shadows between beds. There was a gassy moan. The woman sighed, lying back on the pillow. A tangle of hoses and filaments unwound themselves, groping for her arms and face. Far off, steps began to approach. Conchita looked away.

She turned back to the man beneath the covers. She didn't want to, but there was no help for it.

He was big, and what she could see looked muscular. At first she wondered what he was doing among these invalids, mooncalves and almost-corpses. No wires or tubing seemed to lead to him. Then, off to the side, almost too quickly to see, she saw filaments snake under the covers, discharge some errand and draw back, waiting. His eyes were closed, but she felt he was watching her, like a witch in a story her grandmother told her once, who saw with her eyelids and slept with eyes open. She stared back at the heavy chin, snub nose and bushy eyebrows she'd seen in a thousand vids. When his eyes opened, then narrowed to pin her with his quick, gray eyes, she knew.

"You're Hanrahan," she said.

"Yes, I have been," he agreed.

* * *

Following the Angel, Pilar and Hector found themselves in a long, dimly lit corridor, with evenly spaced doors on either side, all closed. There was a dented aluminum pail a few doors down, with an ordinary wet mop leaning up against the dirty, light blue wall. Pilar stared at it as she passed, not really knowing why.

The Angel seemed to be checking each door as they walked past, reading the numbers and symbols on their pebbled glass windows. She couldn't decipher the symbols and the numbers didn't seem to follow any sequence that Pilar could detect. After the fifth door she lost patience. She was just about to stop him when he grunted and opened the next door, stepping through without waiting to see if she and Hector were following him. He was halfway across a little, disused backyard when she caught up.

Striding past the Angel, she rounded on him, stopping him in his path. "Why are we walking? You and the rest of your New filth just pop out of the air when you want to go somewhere. Why don't you take us to Conchita like that?"

The Angel looked down at her. His skin had gone gray and seemed too big for him now, but he still towered over her. His hands clenched and she knew he wanted nothing more than to wring her neck. "Mujer—""

"No. To you I am Pilar Morales, thing. I have a name."

"Pilar Morales, then. This place is... it changes. If you are one of the Megastars, Silver Orchid or Scimitar or someone like that, you have an updated chart. You know where most things are, the places where Megastars go, anyway. I am not one of the New Ones who has this knowledge, but I could find some of these places and maybe someone who could tell us more.

"But where your daughter has been taken, I think, is not a place the New Stars can find on their own. It isn't on the maps and it isn't a place anyone goes by choice. To get there you have to go to the center and to get to the center you have to walk. Every other path is a detour, a ruse. This is the only way I know to find your Conchita."

Pilar glanced at Hector, who shrugged. She scowled at the Angel.

"Lead on," she said, "but remember the curse I have put upon you."

He nodded and turned. They stepped around a cracked stuccoed corner and were in the New Place.

A long time later, someone once asked Pilar what the New Place looked like the first time she saw it and she couldn't say. It was impossible to keep it all in your eyes at once. There were mountains and cities and rivers and forests and things that didn't have any names Pilar knew. They all seemed to be there at the same time, trees with strange birds you could see right through great fortresses, empty, geometric cities within raging mountain torrents, temples in volcanoes or the other way around. Things changed when you weren't looking. A distant line of dun cliffs was suddenly very close or not there at all. She looked back for the building they'd come from and couldn't spot it, though they'd only gone a dozen paces.

The Angel walked like a drunk going home to someone who would shame and beat him. He lurched past the Church of Fire that perpetually sang the Fugue of Primes, below the flying Web City, through the chambers and vaults of the Skin Mine. It seemed they walked for hours. It was hard to tell.

Just before they got to the mine exit, where they could again see the strange daylight of the New Place, Pilar stopped him again. "Why is this taking so long?" she shouted. The Angel stood mute, eyes on his feet. "I don't want a tour, I want to find my daughter! Is this the only path you know?" The Angel made a sound that could have been yes or no. He seemed to be having difficulty with speech.

Hector, who had been casting wondering glances at Pilar for some time, intervened. "We don't know how big this place is," he said reasonably. "Maybe he doesn't know any faster way than this." The Angel glowered at him, but said nothing.

"He could walk faster. I just-"

"I think everything we have him do hurts him. He walks like a man being whipped. We need him to get us there."

"But-"

"And we don't need to fight anyone. We might, when we get there. Best to save your strength. *Claro*?"

"*Sí.* You're right, Hector."

He watched her steady herself, saw her will her face and shoulders to loosen. She stood straighter, her face quiet, but watchful. I pity Octavio, he thought, if he tries to take this one on when she gets back. If she gets back.

"OK," she said.

"One more thing," he said. "You're watching this guard dog, this Angel, as if your eyes were chained to his back. I think you've made sure he can't run or do us harm. In any case, I will watch him. I think you need to look around. Maybe something you see here will be important. And besides, you may never see the New Place again."

She thought about that, then nodded. "*Es verdad.*" She turned to the Angel, who stood like a ruined, forgotten colossus. "Lead the way," she said, her voice stern. He turned and they stepped out into a valley in the Cloud Mountains that changed, slowly, continuously,

Crawling to the Moon, Page 160

now an elephant, now a ship, now a shape you saw long ago in a dream...

Along the way Pilar and Hector saw a dance of Tornado Fish, children whose words were new galaxies, the WomanCar and her Mechanics. They met Mikhail-7, who laughed at them, and a swarm of logicflies who pestered them with theorems, but most of the New People ignored them.

And after a while Pilar, who had been walking through the New Place like a child to her first communion, began to see that much of what they encountered, at first so strange and different, had a sameness about it. Kiera Who Is Lightning flashed in, out and in of being where Man-Glacier inched ever so slowly, spread over icy miles, but both their eyes had a tepid vacancy that marked them as part of the same listless, waiting crowd. There were others too, people you didn't notice at first among the Megastars of the New Place, ordinary humans like her. Some of them decked themselves out, strutted and posed like discarded sketches for this New One or that. Others avoided her eyes, scuttled away, as if simple humanity were a curse. She glanced over at Hector who, like her, had been wide-eyed as a virgin bride. He was playing with a knife, spinning and whirling it, keeping one eye on the Angel, who shambled ahead of them.

Feeling her eyes upon him, he smiled awkwardly. "*Oye Mamacita*," he said, "How is it a good-looking woman like you doesn't have a man? Where is your little girl's Papa? He should be keeping his child out of places like this." His voice trailed off uncertainly.

Hector, Pilar realized, was a man who could kill in a thousand ways, who had survived brutal, overwhelming attacks and terrible privations. Conversation, though, made him skittish and timid.

"If Rico were here, he'd be more lost than Conchita. Perhaps he is here. I don't know."

"Rico is one of the New Ones?"

"He wanted to be, more than anything. I met him when he was a driver for the McDermotts. He was a handsome man, but not a good driver. Not that he couldn't drive. Somehow he learned how to do that down in Honduras and he was good at it. He didn't know how to do much else, really. He wasn't that good an actor, which is what he always said he was. He was always asking my advice and I told him he should learn a trade while he had work. But he wanted to be New and he couldn't keep his mind on his job. He said the best way to go through the Gate was as a tri-vid star and he was always trying out for parts on the soaps. His English wasn't good, so when he worked he was always a waiter on "*Amigas y Rivales*", a lifeguard on "*Cielo Azul*", things like that. Anyway, he showed up late at the McDermotts once too often and they sacked him. He told me he didn't care, that he had a steady part on "*El Premio Mayor*", but I never saw him there. Someone said she saw him a few years later on a ghost station doing one of those docu-serials. It was about New People who came to Earth to live in an abandoned factory. No one could figure out why they would do this, but it didn't matter, because the people in the show were so obviously crazy with the thought of being New. There was a rumor that it really was broadcast from the New Place, but there are always rumors like that. They said he looked very thin and sick. I felt bad when I heard this, but my friend Lupe said there was nothing I could have done for him."

"Do you miss him?"

"Sometimes. He was sweet sometimes, though he really never thought about anything but being New. He wasn't a bad man, just not as strong as he thought. Or as lucky."

"Luck is a rich man's bed and a poor man's cloud."

"O mi *pobre*. You're alive, you're free and you are where they make the money. Is your luck so bad?

"My luck is what it is. I'm alive after 28 years. That's enough.

"Most boys who want to be gangbangers don't last more than a year. At least my brothers never did."

"I never wanted to join a gang."

"Hector, you are the Chief Enforcer for the Aztec Lords. People talk about you the way they talk about Death. I never want to hear stories about gangs and if half the stories even I've heard are true, you are a fearsome man."

"That may be true, but I never wanted it."

"Then how?"

Hector was silent for a long time. Finally he spoke, sometimes watching the Angel shambling ahead of them, sometimes looking at things only he could see. He spoke the way shy people will sometimes confess to strangers they will never see again, desperately and without restraint. "When I was a boy I lived on a little farm in the foothills of the Sonoras, with my mother, father, an uncle, two aunts, two sisters and three brothers. For cash we grew transgenic potatoes and corn. Vaccines and plastics mostly, a few simple bio-circuits for local manufacturers. There wasn't much money, but we ate well and the local school could afford new data wands and a teacher.

"Then, when I was twelve, we had a bad summer. The rains didn't come in the spring and volcano erupted 20 miles to the south, so the air was full of dust. That year there was a vaccine from the New Place that made the only transgenic potatoes we managed to save worthless. A chromoplague wiped out an expensive strain of circuit corn my father had bought. He was sick too and he died in September.

"The day after my father died, my brothers called me in from the fields for a family meeting. My mother was crying and wouldn't look at me. My oldest brother, Jorge, was the head of the family now. He talked about all the things I told you and he said the farm was bankrupt, that we didn't have enough food to last two weeks.

"But there was a solution, Jorge said. An emissary for some cholos in the US, los Senores Aztec, had approached my family. They had need of a courier, a mule, to bring in a shipment of Shatter. He said it had to be me, for the good of the family."

"Dios mio."

"God wouldn't have anything to do with you once you were on Shatter. The Blessed Virgin would kill anyone in her path, laughing, if she was on Shatter. If they shot out one leg, she'd hop to kill you. If they cut off the other, she'd crawl. I know. I've done it."

"I didn't think anyone came back after taking it."

"Mostly, they don't, but don't believe everything people tell you."

"How did you get it over the border?"

"You only need a tiny bit to get high, even if you're one of the top Tri-vid mercenaries. They put a little bag in me, just under my right lung, that was 10,000 doses. If it had broken, I would have died instantly. They put a needle in my spine too. The doctor said it was just a homing device to guide me in, but I could see my sister's face and I knew he was lying. Then they gave me something to make me sleep. I can vaguely remember them putting a helmet on my head and dressing me in thick, padded clothing, then strapping me into a chair in a concealed compartment on one of those big RVs old gringos drive. Then I passed out.

"When I woke up, it was dark and I was still strapped in the chair. I couldn't see anything but I could feel that the van was on a rough dirt road. I knew we were close to the border, somehow. I also knew I had to go to the purple pulse, though I didn't know what that meant and I didn't remember anyone saying this to me.

"Then there was a little needle stab in my arm. The top of my compartment slammed open and my seat launched itself into the air. The straps holding me in came loose and I was tumbling over and over, pitched like a baseball, a quarter mile without a parachute. It was a moonless, cloudy night but I could see bright as day, from the from my ejection chair exploding and firing off infrared scatter-drones, as the rocks on the ground came up to meet me. I saw the purple pulse, a little black light strobe and I knew I'd smash through anyone or anything that kept me from it. I wasn't afraid, just very, very angry.

"They told me the Border Rangers were on the scene almost immediately and that one got between me and the strobe. He lost his leg up to his knee and never knew how lucky he was. The light was set a hundred feet into an irrigation pipe in the side of a hill. I tore off the welded-on grating and dragged myself to it. It was booby-trapped and when I touched it, I got a dart full of pure heroin and a blast of ether. An Aztec came around a bend in the pipe and shot me with tangle webbing, rolled me up in it and strapped me on the back of a shielded electric dirtbike he drove through the tunnels and hills to Pasadena.

"I don't remember any of this, really, though sometimes I get flashes. The Shatter kicked in before I hit the ground. When I woke up I had a different name. I was in a hospital, up to my neck in a full gel-cast, being fed intravenously. I had broken both legs, my collarbone, jaw, left forearm, and three ribs. Lost four teeth, overdosed and had a concussion. But I had lived, which none of their mules had done before. Cesar, the jefe at the time, said they decided to keep me when I looked at them and said, 'Remember your promise to my family.' That's what he told me I'd said, anyway. I don't remember.

"When I recovered, I found out what they'd shot into my spine was an amygdalic shunt, a self-propagating neural circuit network that controlled my pleasure and pain centers. With it Cesar had his perfect Enforcer. As soon as I could walk they wired up my muscles with extra fast twitch fibre, jacked my response rate off the charts and sent me to school. I learned half a dozen martial arts before I was fifteen. Killing with any weapon, torture, bombs, reconnaissance, they taught me everything they could think of. With the shunt, Cesar played me like a guitar, punishing me with excruciating pain, never the same twice, if I didn't work hard enough, showering me with unspeakable pleasure when I performed. I was his shunt-slave, his terrible little lapdog."

"Why go to all this trouble and expense? Gangboy killers are cheap enough."

Hector paused, considering. "I think I was his hobby. In a way, Cesar was kind of a hacker. He wanted to see just how deadly he could make any one human being. He was always upgrading me with sensing and jamming capabilities, nano-wires, blades, you name it. Plus, the word about me got around. At first, that brought all the machos with a name to make. I killed a few of them, which made others reconsider. Then the Lords started sending me on missions. A few times they cleaned me up, bleached my hair, put me in a little girl's dress and sent me to a rival gang clubhouse where I'd kill almost everyone in five minutes with my bare hands. After that, no one challenged the Aztec Lords. They had expanded past Pasadena and were making inroads into East LA, when Octavio took over."

"How did that happen, when Cesar had you?"

"Octavio found the guy who encrypted my control box, which Cesar had grafted into his shoulder. He bribed him or threatened him, I don't know which, but he got the code. Then he waited till Cesar went to bed one night, overrode his control and put me in a trance where I sat at the foot of Cesar's bed. Then he walked in, woke me electronically, explained what I had to do and threw the switch. It took two seconds. It never even woke Cesar's girlfriend, and she was sleeping right beside him."

"Does that make you feel bad?"

"Bad, no. I traded one puppeteer for another, that's all. Octavio is not as good an administrator as a Cesar and he's lazy, so oftentimes there's nothing for me to do. He thinks I study killing and all the rest and sometimes I do. But I've used the time to piece together what has happened to me and what I have done. Some day there will be a Law and the people who serve the Law will want to know these things."

Crawling to the Moon, Page 165

"Why did Octavio send you with me, if you are his most powerful weapon?"

"If I come back with something good, then he's rich and the Aztec Lords will be feared and respected. Our stock has been falling since he took over, because he doesn't know how to run the rackets like Cesar did. Also, other gangs have shunt-slaves now, some with better mods than me. Octavio has a new one too, a boy named Esteban, whom he's bringing up from Guadelajara. He doesn't think I know, but that's my replacement right now, if I don't come back. Or in a few years, if I do."

"But what's to stop you from coming back with something good and selling it to the highest bidder? Or using it against Octavio?"

"I have always followed orders."

"And what are your orders, Hector?"

"My orders are to find something good, steal it and come back with it and the Coin."

"What about helping me find Conchita?"

"Octavio doesn't care about that."

"And why haven't you? We've seen all kinds of things the Aztec Lords could use or sell."

"I don't know the way back."

"You could make someone take you."

"Maybe. I don't know, maybe there's something more than what I've seen. Maybe I've been wasting time. It's just that someone once told me something I needed to do. It's silly, probably."

"Tell me."

"It's stupid."

"No, really, I want to know."

He looked at her doubtfully and Pilar realized that for the first time in many years, Hector was concerned about what someone else thought. She suddenly wanted to cradle him in her arms, to stroke his jaguar hair.

"You won't laugh?"

"I promise."

"When I was eight years old," he said slowly, "I got very sick. I ran a fever, couldn't breathe, couldn't hold food down. The doctor in the next village couldn't help me. He said there were drugs from the New Place that might work. But they were very expensive, more than we made all year. And even then, he said, I still might die. Everyone thought I would be gone in a few days. The priest came over to visit, ready to say last rites.

"But I wasn't there. During the night my mother took one of the burros, loaded me and some food and blankets on it and set off into the mountains to Dona Esmerelda, an old woman who was supposed to be a very powerful *bruja*. She didn't tell anyone she was going, because they didn't believe in that sort of thing and my brother Rodrigo, who wanted to be a priest, would have stopped her. I think my father knew, maybe.

"I don't remember much of the trip there. I was delirious most of the time. I do remember there was a wild ram's horn with the tip sawed off hanging from a joshua tree that grew in the box canyon she lived in. My mother blew it like a trumpet and all of the sudden the *bruja* was there.

"She was old, very old and she didn't speak much Spanish. Her face was tattooed and her white braids came down to her knees. I remember she wore jeans and a man's shirt. In our village only gringo women wore anything but dresses. She looked into my eyes, sniffed me all over, even licked my forehead. Then she drew mi Madre aside. I guess they talked about a price. It must have been something my mother cared about, but she never told me what.

"The next thing I remember is being hauled in a sling up the gold and red side of the canyon, with the hot winds blowing me this way and that. The witch's house was carved into the sandstone canyon wall, like the homes of the old ones, the Anansi. She had rigged up a block and tackle in her cave hut. How she and my mother kept from knocking my brains out on the rocks, I don't know.

"My mother said the witch put her to work then, gathering this herb or that mushroom, trapping little lizards, stealing eggs from birds. She said later she was never sure which ones the *bruja* used to heal me and which ones she just wanted. Every few hours she would chant something in a language I never heard before and rub something into my skin.

"After a few days the *bruja* sent my mother away, back to her family. She said I would either die or get better. It was up to me.

"I got better. But first my fever ran so high that when it broke, I couldn't speak. I had forgotten the words of man, but as soon as I could eat solid food, I grew rapidly stronger. In a day I was up and walking. In a week, I was out all day and most of the night, climbing

Crawling to the Moon, Page 167

the gold and red canyon wall like a goat, running with the wild mountain sheep, following the coyotes to their lairs.

"Dona Esmerelda had to lure me to the cave with food, had to teach me to speak again by rewarding me with a tortilla only when I repeated words after her. She taught me her language and such Spanish as she knew. She taught me how to charm a jaguar with a song, use a burrowing owl's feather against your enemies and how to track water when it hid.

"I stayed with her for maybe three months, until every night you'd hear booming as the cactuses fired their seeds off in the moonlight. She sent me off with a sheep-herder, a great-nephew of hers, back to my family. I didn't want to go, but before I left she drew a design on my forehead with a special salve she made and cast my prophecy stones. She told me it was not my destiny to be a *brujo* or a farmer. She said I had been a child and a beast and that before I died I would be a slave, a soldier and a king in a far-off place. Then she gave me something to make me sleep before I could run away into the mountains. When I woke up I was strapped to the back of a big goat, just around the bend from my family's farm.

When the sheep-herder and I walked into the farmyard, the whole family stopped what they were doing and came out. My mother ran to take me in her arms, but the rest of them stayed back. I was thin and almost two inches taller than the boy they remembered. My hair was long and my sister said I had heathen symbols painted on my face. It took me a few days before I could converse easily in Spanish. But they put me to work and back into school. In a little while I'd almost forgotten where I had been."

"You remember now."

"Yes. But I have my orders."

"But you also have what Dona Esmerelda told you."

"That's true. If it all wasn't a dream. A few years ago, I had a mission, a shipment out of my home state to guard. There was a delay, so I used the time to go back to the box canyon. There are expensive homes there now and an artificial lake where retired German and Chinese executives fish for bass. Nothing looked like I remembered it. No one knew anything about a *bruja*."

"But you remember it."

"The things I've done, the drugs they've given me and the changes they've made... I think maybe I make things up to make myself feel better, sometimes."

They walked in silence for a while. Finally Pilar said, "So Octavio is counting your loyalty, even though he means to replace you."

"He knows where my family is. He doesn't know that I know mi Madre is dead and that she was the only one I cared for. Really, though, he thinks I don't remember being free. He thinks I'm a pistol, not comfortable except in a holster or being shot."

"And are you?"

Hector finally looked her in the eyes. "I don't know," he said.

They walked on for a while. Suddenly Hector turned to Pilar as if seeing her for the first time. "*Oye, Mamacita*," he said, "what's your story?"

"What do you mean?"

"I mean you're a poor woman, working for rich gringos who can't be bothered to get you full status, who called the Popcops on you--"

He grinned and shook his head ruefully when she stared at him sharply. "Ai mujer, did you think because you kept yourself ignorant of us, that los Senores didn't know about you? Pilar, we're your friend's brothers, your nephews and cousins. When a temp secretary steals a paperclip, we know about it. And we watch everything going in and out of Harvest concessions especially."

She faced him stonily, willing her rage and shame down. She wouldn't let this gangboy see her pain and surprise. "Go on," she said, with a voice that shook, though quietly.

He seemed surprised at how he'd hurt her, contrite. "You were born poor," he said, not meeting her eyes, "and you'll die poor, most likely. Your daughter's in the New Place. Maybe they're making her a Megastar, a New One, as we speak. Maybe she's eating better than you could ever feed her, meeting important New People, dancing on other planets, making Tri-Vids. Many mothers would kill to give their children that chance. But you want to take her back to Santa Esperanza, to live poor, with poor women like you and men like me." He glanced at her. "You don't seem like one of those hag-mothers who wants to hang on her child like a leech or steal what she's got. But you want her back with you in the shithole we come from. What's your story?"

"I don't have a story."

"Everyone has a story."

"I don't. Stories are for people who never,,," She trailed off.

"Go on."

"I don't know what to say."

"Hey, I told you all that loco shit about myself." He nodded toward the Angel, reeling like a lame drunk front of them as they walked through a vast, dun plain. It seemed they had left the wonders of the New Place behind. For a long time now they'd been walking through spiky dry grass, theirs the only tracks they could see. Sometimes they came on a ditch, sometimes a lone tree. But mostly flat tan prairie in the strange harsh sunlight of the New Place, as far as the eye could see. "I think we've got time."

She frowned, but nodded. At length, she spoke. "My mother always told me my father was a famous Tri-Vid mercenary, a champion, Alejandro Cortes. Maybe you've heard of him?"

At Hector's blank look, she nodded. "They don't stay famous long, those ones. Anyway, she said he was my father and that someday he would come and take us away, back to Los Angeles, where I was born. We lived in one of those plastic bubble pueblos in the *maquiladora* just outside San Fernando. She had a job in a factory that made liquid crystal displays." Another blank look from Hector and she smiled. "I don't think they make them any more since everyone got Tri-Vid. She, my two little brothers and me, we all ate and slept in the same little room. And there were pictures of Alejandro Cortes all over the walls. Souvenirs from his fights, pictures of him in the ring, pictures of him with his wife with her head covered over with a cut-out picture of *mi Madre*'s face. She wrote long letters to him, back when they still delivered paper mail and she had ways of finding out his e-mail address, or that's what she told us. She was always talking about him.

"And one day it came to me. My mother did not notice her life. All she could see was this story she'd put together from old TV and Tri-Vid, paper magazines and chatgroups, this story where she and Alejandro were married and living some life with details that kept changing. She barely saw my brothers and me, the little smelly plastic bubble we lived in, the factory where she worked 12 hour shifts.

"Once she even got us in to his dressing room to see him, before his last fight, in LA. I don't know how she did it. Maybe he really was my father. I remember a room at the end of a dark cement corridor, stinking of blood, disinfectant and smoke, full of nervous men who shouted a lot.

"I never saw my mother more beautiful than in there. All these sweating, swearing men, ready to jump out of their skins and there she sat, smiling and glowing like the Blessed Virgin. It was like this was the only place she was really real.

"The mercenary, Alejandro, seemed like he barely saw my mother or anything else. He was like you, all muscles and scars. Bigger, though. His eyes rolled like a cow in the killing line and he gave little nervous nods to everything his trainer said. I thought, this can't be my father. My father is calm and rich. Once or twice he glanced over at my mother and us. It looked like he tried to say something, but got interrupted by something else in his head. Too much Shatter, I guess.

"While they were strapping him into his armor and checking over his weapons, I looked over at his dressing table and the trunks they carried his equipment in. They were covered, completely covered in pictures of other Tri-Vid mercs, the ones who'd gone over, who'd been picked out and become New. Suddenly I knew he was like her. All they knew was these stories they'd made up out of stories other people had made up for them. They couldn't see or hear anything else. They were numb and they couldn't smell the stench of that room. Most of all they didn't notice three small children watching them, waiting for someone to be their Madre y Padre.

"We stayed and watched the fight, though it wasn't something children should see, especially not right up by the Octagon Cage, where we were sitting. It was Alejandro's last one, the one where he died. He was actually winning when it happened. He'd sliced through his opponent's bungee line and broken the man's knee. He had his chainsword out and was stalking his man, wearing him down, getting ready for the kill.

"He passed by us and my mother called out. Suddenly he stopped. He looked at us, really looked at us, my mother, my brothers and me. He looked over at the other side of the Octagon, where his wife was sitting. He looked at the big cage he was in, spattered with blood in the middle, surrounded by screaming, cursing, loveless strangers. He looked at the Tri-Vid monitors. They were all hovering in the crowd because they had noticed a New One sitting there, Draco McKenzie, I think. He looked at these things and then he turned the chainsword on himself. He tore himself to pieces, but he never said a thing."

"Now that you tell me," Hector said, "I do remember hearing about this man."

"My mother was silent on the way home. My little brothers were weeping, but not me. The next morning she woke us up for school, same as usual. Nothing had changed. Tomorrow, she said, our father was going to pick us up after school and we'd go horseback riding. Wouldn't that be fun?

"My little brother Roberto, who was seven, started screaming that Papa was dead, dead and Luis, just turned five, began crying. I didn't say anything, because I knew nothing we said could reach her. But I decided there and then that I wasn't going to live in someone else's story.

"And I never have. I knew Gabriella, the McDermott's maid before me. She was always scheming, coming up with ways to get through the Portal and into the New Place, where she'd be a Star. She ate, drank and slept being New, except she wasn't. Maybe she even got over. I think we might have seen her, back by the Church of Fire. Whoever it was was in a maid's uniform and she hid her face from me, like she was ashamed.

"Me, I do the cleaning and ironing, same as Gabriella. But when I'm cleaning I notice the sunlight coming in through the windows and I can tell by the angle what time it is, and by the catbird singing in the garden. I do the ironing and I smell the difference between linen and cotton, listen to the hiss of the iron, the way the cloth's colour changes a tiny bit when it's flattened. I call Conchita and I can tell by the way she smells and answers that she is having her first period and she is scared and proud. All these New Ones and the people who want to be New, they do this and that, they have their stories. But they don't smell their lives, feel them on their skin, taste them. And their children are dead to them."

"But now," Hector said, nodding at the flock of Tri-Vids flying toward them, "you have a story too."

Pilar nodded grimly. One of them hovered in front of her and Silver Orchid's projection appeared in it. "Pilar Morales," the tiny head in the silver ball said, "you've come to the New Place with your gangboy lover, in search of your daughter Conchita, overcoming countless dangers and setbacks. How does it feel?"

When Pilar didn't answer, Silver Orchid asked the question again. Again she was silent and the Tri-Vid kept asking the question, phrased exactly the same, as if it were on a computer loop. Finally Pilar looked into the lens and said "How does it feel? It feels like a buzzard has me down, tearing my guts out and once in a while asking me how it feels."

Hector grinned, caught the ball in both hands and quickly squeezed it till it popped in a shower of thin glassy stuff and circuitry. The Tri-Vids kept their distance after that and they walked on.

As they traveled the Angel got more and more agitated. Sometimes he pleaded with them to release him, in a voice growing harder and harder to understand, like metal scraping metal. Once they caught him trying to rub the token off on the trunk of a Growl Tree. Pilar reminded him then, in a low, deadly voice, of the curse she had put on him. He shuddered and grew quiet, like a man waking on his deathbed. But mostly he shambled wordlessly ahead, white pants and shirt fading to ragged gray skin over a flattened oblong body, while Pilar watched him carefully and Hector scanned for danger and something to steal.

At last they came to a place like a great split hoof mark in the middle of the vastness of parched dun grass. The sun seemed the wrong colour, though you couldn't tell exactly how. The wind was icy and smelled old. The soil in the hoof mark was the colour of half-dried blood.

"Lie down here," said the Angel. At least, that's what he seemed to be saying, pointing to the matched teardrops of bare red earth. His voice was hard to make out, high and metallic.

"Where is Conchita?" said Pilar. "Take me to her!"

"Here!" grated the Angel. "Here!" His edges seemed to flicker and Hector could tell he was not just frustrated, but fearful. "Lie down here!" he repeated.

Pilar looked around. "I don't trust him," she said to Hector.

Hector looked at the Angel, considering. "Maybe you should do as he says," he suggested, "while I watch him."

"OK." Not taking her eyes off the grayish, wavering giant, Pilar said evenly, "If something goes wrong, or if you feel something bad has happened, do what you can to this one."

"Claro. If I can, I will follow."

Pilar looked at him full in the face. "As you will, Hector. If you can't make it, don't let my daughter and me be unavenged. This is all I ask of you." He nodded.

Crawling to the Moon, Page 173

She sat down on the bare earth, then stretched out on her back. Nothing happened. Pilar closed her eyes and folded her hands.

Then, from somewhere, came a sound, half birdsong, half cough. A moaning dry wind sprang up. The Angel loosed a snarling, electric scream and Hector pivoted towards him, hands ready. In that moment, Pilar shouted "Conchita! I see you! I'm coming!" and the thirsty red earth swallowed her like dew, without a trace, before Hector could even move.

Chapter Six

Conchita and Hanrahan stared at each other silently, like two shy dinner companions who'd come alone to a party where they knew no one. Hanrahan cleared his throat a couple of times, as if he meant to talk, but to Conchita it seemed as if the man had lost the knack of conversation, or even speaking beyond a few words. All the while, she could hear footsteps, approaching their corner of the big room.

"I want to go home," she said.

Hanrahan seemed to have forgotten she was there. Something small, moving too fast to focus on, zippered down a flap of skin in his neck. A flash of dark veins, scarlet artery, pinkish gristle, tiny blue and green filaments, and he was sewn up again. She couldn't even see the seam. His mouth hung slack, as if waiting for someone to close it. The steps were getting closer.

Conchita was hungry and tired. She leaned toward him, grabbed his sleeve. "I want to go home!" she repeated.

Hanrahan stared blankly at her. Slowly, his eyes focussed. "Why would you want to do that?" he asked mildly. The footsteps paused.

"I want to be with my mother."

He frowned, as if such a thing had never occurred to him. Then he brightened. "We can bring your mother here to live with you."

Conchita looked around at the vast room, its dim corners and harsh lights, the winking, humming machines, dank floors, the bodies strapped down, wired up, gibbering, tumbling inside restraint fields, the smells of decay, human and alien. "I don't want you to bring her here."

"This is only one tiny part of the New Place. We could go wherever you liked."

"Why you stay here? I thought New People don't get sick."

"I'm not sick. I brought you here, remember?"

Crawling to the Moon, Page 175

"You did not! It was--" She turned. The Woman with Red Chains lay inertly on the bed she had occupied, face covered by a spiky orange mask. The woman's chest was split open from breastbone to sternum. A creature like a translucent monkey had pulled out her liver and was tucking it into a cavity in its chest. When this was done, the monkey dived under the next bed. It didn't emerge.

"That was once Dimanche," said Hanrahan. "Did you notice? Maybe a bit before your time."

"I know about Dimanche."

"So she's been renewed, eh? I thought she was a keeper. Of course, she was me before. Maybe will be again, hmmm? All of them here," he swept his arm to encompass the whole space, "they're all me. More or less."

Conchita had heard that some of the New People had different bodies, but she'd never known what that meant, exactly. "They can't all be you.

Why not?" said Hanrahan, sounding like Mr. McDermott when he was teasing her, just before he tried to put his hand in her pants.

She edged away, slightly. "A lot of them aliens, man. A lot of them dead."

"Around here, alien and dead don't mean very much. This place wouldn't be here, if it weren't for alien dead people. Now you take, um..." he gestured toward the bed down the hall.

Conchita looked. The Woman with Red Chains was gone. "Where'd she go? Did that thing--"

"You see, that's just what I'm getting at: The Phage Ape is as much me as the one who used to be Dimanche." He frowned again. "How to explain it? You know about cytology?"

She stared at him blankly. Her mother had gotten her some edu-disks, but they were an old format and hard to use on their skoolcomp. An old woman in Santa Esperanza was teaching her how to read, but it was slow, compared to talking to the McDermott's datawand.

"Cells? In your body?"

"Oh sure. Everyone knows your body got cells." Conchita remembered the datawand had told her about this and shown MRI animations when she asked about someone in the village who had cancer. It wouldn't tell her where she could get medicine, though.

"Y'see, instead of just cells in my body, I have. . . uh, suppose I want to go to where--you see that sort of knobby fish guy over there? Suppose I want to go to where it's from. Well, I just slip on that body and-"

"Why don't you just go?"

"I do just go."

"But in your own body. Instead of another one."

"Well, you see, he lives in an ocean of liquid methane, cold enough to freeze you or me solid in a minute. A little girl like you would weigh half a tonne on his planet."

"Put on a spacesuit."

"That's what the body is for me. A spacesuit."

"But wasn't there someone inside it before?"

"That body? Maybe. I don't remember. If there was, it's here with me. Nothing is lost here. Everyone here is me. And I'm everyone."

"You're not me. I'm me."

"Except for you. Well, that will change." The footsteps began to advance again. Conchita turned around, but the room was blurring in front of her eyes. She couldn't tell who or what was coming, or how many there were. There was a tingling at her wrist. She looked down, saw the almost invisibly thin tubule snaking from it, slapped it away. It prickled, but suddenly things were clearer.

She turned to Hanrahan, who regarded her with a mild, connoisseur's interest. She knew she couldn't run or fight them. "Why do you want me? I'm just a poor ground girl. I'm no one. I'm nothing."

"Sometimes I like to walk in the barrio. Drink cheap pulque. Listen to maids gossip."

"But you could do all those things! You don't need me! You're an earth person--at least you were! Why not go yourself?"

"Oh, I couldn't do that."

"Why not?"

"Well, um, this is the, uh, original soma. It's got priceless archival value. Say if there was some chromoplague or such--and every once in a while they do happen--you're going to need some original tissue. Besides," he smiled, "I tend to be a bit careless with bodies." The footsteps got closer. Conchita could see dark wires homing in on her, gray, oblong shapes rising through the floor, leaning in...

She turned to him. "How can you do this, man?" They were almost upon her...

"A long time ago, I made a deal with people who do this sort of thing all the time." A hand like a star of needles reached for her...

* * *

"Where did she go? Where did you send her?" Hector yelled, advancing on the Angel, hands at ready.

Oddly, the Angel appeared to be recuperating. Already he was more substantial, more human-looking. "You heard her, Earther. She went to join her daughter."

"Are they alive? Are they free? Tell me!"

The Angel sighed. "Gangboy, listen to me. I am not the one you need to ask. Do you think I stand at the door, like a porter, dealing with any piece of trash some New brat takes a fancy to, because I am powerful and respected here? There are many things no one who knows bothers to tell me. All I know is that they're together."

"Can you tell me where--"

"If you want to know more, you must lie in the cleft yourself."

Hector looked at the red earth crescent. "Si, I guess you're right. Well, there's only one thing left to do." He reached for the blue token embedded in the Angel's forehead.

The Angel drew back. "But you'll need me to guide you back to the Door. Come back and I'll show you the way." He turned to go.

"I'm not going back."

"What do you mean, you're not going back? You can't stay here. They'd hunt you down and exterminate you." His face was weighted with concern.

"I'm hard to kill."

"But what about the loot you wanted? If you left now, before too many of the New Ones knew about you, you could have as much as you could carry. I could show you weapons, drugs--"

Hector lifted his wrists so fine silver wires glinted in the alien light. "And return to a Jefe who keeps my will bound up in a net? Steal for him, kill for him, till someone younger and better wired tears me apart? No thanks." He reached again for the sapphire coin, now glowing dully.

The Angel knocked his hand aside. He towered over Hector, his chest a boulder, arms and legs tree trunks. "Leave it," he said in a ground-shaking basso. "Somehow, I'm used to it now."

Hector nodded, then swept the Angel's feet out from under him. His spinning roundhouse kick snapped the huge head back. "Now I think I must insist." He gripped the token firmly this time--

The return blow knocked him off his feet. He landed, stunned, on his back.

"Fool! Once I have completed the exchange, the Coin is mine!" The Angel's voice was seismic. He lumbered to his feet.

"Why did you fight us, then?" Hector winced and gripped his wrist, bent at an odd angle.

"The Designers laid a ban upon our kind, one this errand has broken."

"Then you and I are slaves alike."

"For that, groundscum, I will pop your spine like a bean pod, joint by joint." And on he came, a swaggering colossus, huge hands reaching.

Hector gave ground as slowly as possible, but his punches and kicks seemed to have no effect and the knives he used just stuck wherever he slashed and stabbed without slowing his adversary. His right arm managed one last, strange flinging motion and his left hand closed before the Angel caught him as a man traps a kitten. Giant hands tore at his shoulders, jerking, wrenching...

Abruptly, the Angel's grip faltered. He slapped at the back of his neck and his hand came back dripping yellowish ichor. Hector kicked him in the chest. Pulled by the gangboy's weight, the taut nanowire looped from his wrist sheared the Angel's head off like a huge gourd. It fell with a dull thud, coming to rest in a clump of stiff grass, a few yards from the stumbling, toppling body.

Hector gasped a few times, then lay still till his heart had slowed. Slowly he rolled over and gingerly got to his feet, favouring his right side.

A rustle made him turn.

The huge body was climbing to its feet, staggering toward him. The head had pitched face up, eyes rolling to include him in the joke. "You can't stop me that way, gangboy," it sneered, words coming in lungless gasps.

But when Hector gripped the gleaming coin again, the Angel screamed, a next-to-soundless shriek. He tackled the snapping, spasming head, twisting and yanking the token off and out, trailing a wet, rooty tangle of nerves and wires. Almost upon him, the titan crumpled in a stinking hiss, like a dry-rotted tree.

The dun plain bristled, humming with tiny blue sparks, like thin insulation over a vast circuit. Things not truly clouds raced toward the off-spectrum sun. Strange thunder scraped in the distance.

Hector stuffed the coin, now seething with light, into his pocket, barely registering the knotted wires and nerves that had fallen from it in a shrunken, powdery heap. Spiky sensors glittering in his raised forearms, he turned like a searching mantis, this way and that, sampling airwaves. He felt a confluence of frequencies, data streams too fast and complex to decode, converging on this place. It flowed through him, past his eyes and over his nerves till his head ached and belly was sick with it. He could feel the integers racing through his wiring, as they searched for his control code. He retracted his sensors, but that made scant difference.

Something was coming. Far off, the plain's edges were flickering, fading, losing material coherence. There were lights in every direction, like the Angel when they first saw it, gliding toward him.

Hector sighed and turned back to the teardrop of bare, red earth. Then he stopped. He leaped over to where the Angel's inert carcass lay, yanking a knife out of its side and wiping it clean on his pants. Then he turned it on the silvery wires in his skin, slashing and prying, biting his tongue against the pain, like a man skinning himself. The lights drew nearer. He watched them while he measured the distance to the bare earth teardrop. Still he sliced and hacked.

* * *

Comment

The premise of The New People is simple. It postulates a world like ours, obsessed with celebrity, where the rich and connected are functionally exempt from real consequences that apply to you and me, should we lie, abuse, swindle or make catastrophically bad decisions depriving others of their lives, health and livelihoods. But in addition to the web of slanted laws, bought-off politicians, tax shelters, insider deals, armies of lawyers and soldiers that protect them in our world, the

New People also live in the New Place, a dimension protected by science so advanced as to be essentially magic.

A word about my protagonist. In Pilar, what I was aiming for someone with the peculiar mix of intimacy, access and legal powerlessness that undocumented immigrant servants experience in the homes of the rich and powerful who employ them. As a maid, Pilar is in a hyper-adult position relative to her charges, the McDermotts. She sees them at their worst, their most infantile and helpless. She could easily, should she so desire, sabotage their household or do them irreparable harm. At the same time, legally she is the very definition of a chattel, a person without rights or recourse, dependent on the whims and mercy of her employers.

Of course there's a problem here: I am neither female, born poor, nor Latina. But it's the problem inherent in any choice to tell or read a story through the eyes and words of anyone but yourself. If you have the temerity to do that, you are already in the cross-hairs of people whose only response to art is to count and rate, not to understand, and certainly not to create. We are fixed in history, bound up in class, gender and language, trapped within our all too limited senses, minds and skins. Any empathy we have for others is first and foremost, an act of imagination. All I ask is for my work to be judged individually rather than on a programmatic basis.

The End

Crawling to the Moon, Page 182

ABOUT THE AUTHOR

Scott Ellis

Scott Ellis has been a door-to-door salesman, professional malingerer, show groom, bonsai lumberjack, phone interviewer, arts scene curmudgeon, peculiarly well-rated credit risk, freelance ontologist and entrance-level maladroit for many years now.

Also by Scott Ellis

BENNY THE ANTICHRIST

A hilarious and thought provoking collection of stories and vignettes from noted science fiction and fantasy storyteller, Scott Ellis, featuring:

Benny the Antichrist, *He's the arch-arch-villain, the most made guy in this universe or any other.*

The Reason of Sleep, *A world ruled by those who never sleep and those who live in dreams?*

Fae-Dar, *A bar full of gods, trolls and pixies…in walks an accountant.*

In the Shaft, *Getting high and playing ball in a skyscraper elevator shaft.*

Saccade, *He's under no illusions, That's his big problem.*

Magic Phone, *About guns, long distance and neutrinos*

The Deep Crew, *who handles the psychic garbage of an entire city?*

"Scott Ellis is an excellent writer with a penchant for sophisticated, intelligent themes manifested through realistic, complex characterization. And sometimes he writes just for fun. This collection, exhibits a pleasing variety of the output of his intense imagination. Overall, quite a treat to read."

R, Graeme Cameron, Amazing Stories Magazine

FOSSIL COVE PUBLISHING

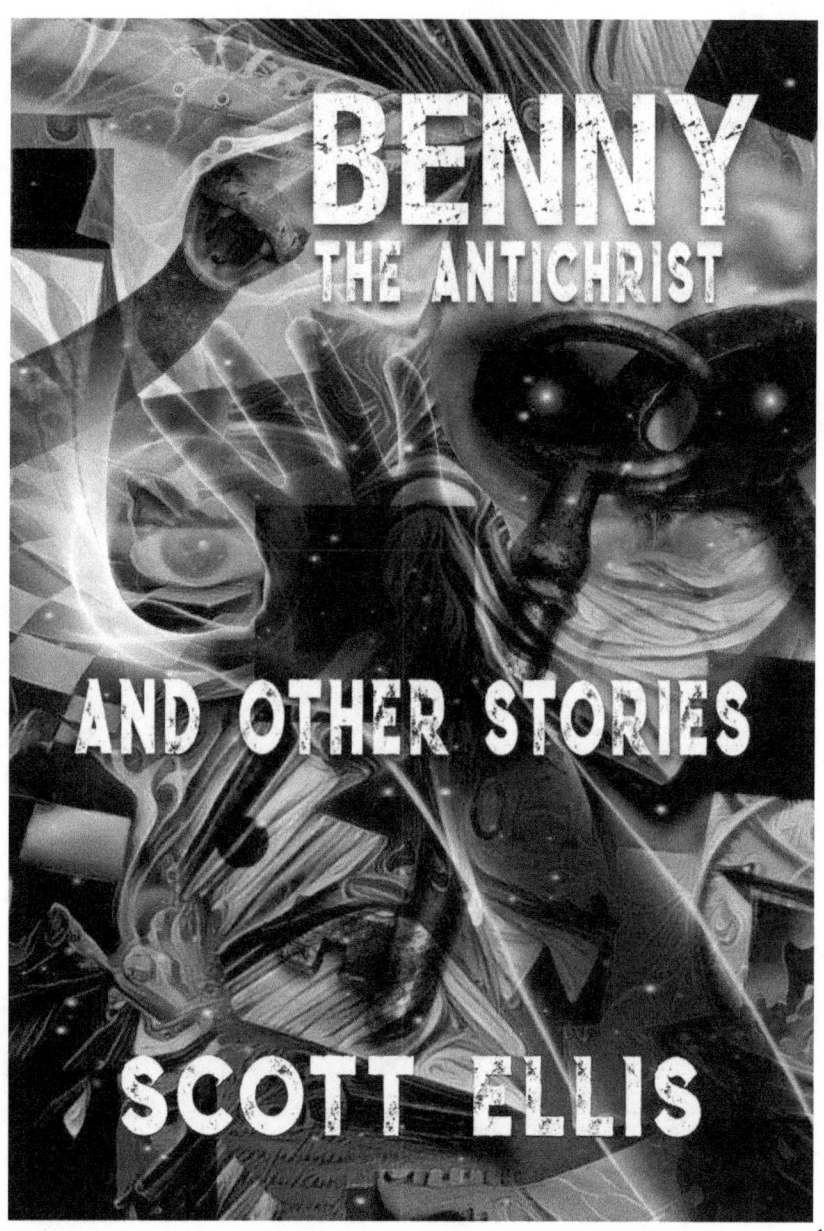

Crawling to the Moon, Page 185